CIRQUE AND THE *SHADOW* CHASERS

BY BROOKLYNN LANGSTON

Printed in the United States of America

2021 First Edition

10 9 8 7 6 5 4 3 2 1

Subject Index:

Langston, Brooklynn

Title: Cirque and the Shadow Chasers

1. Middle School Fiction 2. Fantasy 3. Schools 4. Bullying

Library of Congress Card Catalog Number: 2021924593

Langston Publishing

Langstonpublishing.com

Ourcirque.com

FOR YOU.

THIS BOOK IS FOR ANYONE
WHO HAS EVER FELT ALONE.
ANYONE WHO EVER WANTED
TO ESCAPE. ANYONE WHO
JUST NEEDED SOMEONE TO
CARE.

I HOPE THIS BOOK FEELS LIKE
HOME. I HOPE IT SHOWS
YOU THAT LIFE IS GOOD
AND SO WORTH LIVING.

B Longer

CONTENTS

PART ONE

1. R.L.

"**K**nock, knock." The ringleader looked up as his assistant, and best friend, Barnaby, entered the office. Barnaby stood in front of the old wooden desk and glanced out of the massive round window behind it.

"Who's there?" R.L. asked with a raised eyebrow. He closed the thick leather-bound book he had been thumbing through and stood up from his chair.

"Destiny, apparently," Barnaby replied with a smile. He tossed his gold pocket watch slightly in the air and caught it, repeating this motion several times—it was a habit of his.

"As usual," R.L mused.

Barnaby watched as his friend put on his dark purple peacoat and dusted off one of his top hats he hadn't worn in a while. The navy blue material was slightly tattered but its tiny silver stars still twinkled marvelously.

R.L. whistled a cheerful tune while glancing around his office for a particular journal. He grunted in approval once his eyes landed on the worn red leather nestled on a bookshelf. After flipping through pages and pages of scribbled names, he finally stopped on one. His finger glided over the ink and he smiled. It was almost time.

Together, R.L. and Barnaby walked through the hallways of Cirque Des Élus towards their destination. They greeted their performers as they passed them—jugglers, clowns, the snake family.

"This next bunch," Barnaby spoke as they walked down a hallway lined with shelves that were filled with knick-knacks. "Are you sure they're the ones to help?" He had to admit. He had slight doubts that such a job could be trusted with the group they were about to bring in.

R.L answered with a wink and a lopsided grin, "It's always the most fun when it's the most surprising."

2. JAIDEN

Jaiden took a deep breath. He raised his leg, rolled his shoulder once, and then threw the baseball as if his life depended on it. His teammate struck out and Jaiden smirked, proud of his pitch.

"Nice work, Jaiden!" His coach called before going to the batter to give him tips.

"You're gonna get us that win, Jaiden," Corey called from third base.

Jaiden laughed at his best friend's comment and replied, "I'm counting on it."

Practice went on a little while longer, with Jaiden pitching perfectly every time, which was no surprise to his team or anyone watching from the metal bleachers. Jaiden was good at everything he did, on the baseball diamond and off of it.

"Alright, boys, see you at the game this weekend. Rest up," coach told them.

Sitting in the dugout, Jaiden changed out of his cleats and gulped down a sports drink. He checked his phone to see a text from his mom and his girl friend, Sophia. Yes, girl-friend, with a space in between. He was hoping to close that space on their date tonight, though.

"We're getting pizza. You down?" Corey asked as they walked away from the field.

"Can't. Gotta get home and get ready for my date," Jaiden told him, trying to hide how nervous he was.

"Oh yeah, finally gonna ask Sophia to be your girlfriend," Corey said louder than Jaiden would have liked.

"Yea, but shut up." Jaiden pushed Corey's shoulder lightly.

"And then you're gonna' make out with her, sounds way more fun than pizza." Despite Jaiden pushing him again, Corey continued to make obnoxious kissing sounds.

Jaiden laughed, "I don't know about all that."

"Someone's nervous!" Corey teased.

"Shut up," Jaiden adjusted the ball cap on his head. "See ya."

"I wanna hear details later!" Corey hollered as they walked opposite directions.

As Jaiden walked home he thought about what was making him the most nervous about the date—his parents. He was the oldest of three, the only boy, and hadn't ever had a girlfriend before. He never kept anything from his parents, but he was going to take his time telling them about Sophia.

It wasn't that they were against him having a girlfriend, but they were always talking about how he needs to stay focused on school. There wasn't a day that went by that they didn't discuss the future, whether it was Jaiden's or one of his sisters'.

'We came to this country so you could have the opportunities we never had.' That was his mom's favorite line. Every day he was

reminded of the millions of sacrifices his parents had made to give him and his sisters a better life.

Dad would probably say that having a girlfriend is a distraction, he thought. But, he wanted to have a life, a little fun before his future started. From the way his parents talked, the future would be a lot of work, but it's what he had to do. *For them, I have to work hard. For them.*

He closed his front door behind him and kicked off his slides. He could hear his mom in the kitchen making dinner and his sisters in the living room doing homework. His dad was probably still on his way home from work.

He quickly showered and changed, taking longer than ever to pick out what to wear. "It's just a freaking T-shirt," he mumbled to himself.

His phone vibrated on his dresser and he checked to see a text from Sophia; *Can't wait to see you,* with the blushing emoji. He sent back, *same,* with the winky face and a gif of some guy dancing. He smiled when she sent back laughing faces.

"Jaiden?" his mother called.

"Coming!" He replied. He put his phone in his pocket, grabbed the test he had gotten back in school that day out of his backpack, and went downstairs.

"Hey," he said as he entered the kitchen. He kissed his mother on the cheek.

She smiled. "You look nice." She looked him up and down and then sniffed him. "And smell nice. Where are you going?" She raised an eyebrow.

This was it. *Do I lie? Do I tell the truth?* Maybe he could tell her about Sophia and then show her the 100 on his test.

Maybe it would convince her that he's very focused and no girl would ruin that. The front door opening and closing snapped him out of his train of thought. *This just got way harder.* It was always more difficult convincing his dad of anything.

After saying hi to the girls, Jaiden's dad came into the kitchen and greeted him and his mom. "Are you going somewhere?" he asked after looking at his son for a minute.

"That's what I was asking," Jaiden's mom joined in. They both stared at him waiting for an answer.

"I was hoping that after dinner I could go hang out with the guys at the park," the words tumbled out of his mouth before he could stop them. *Guess I'm lying then.*

"Why are you dressed so fancy if it's only gonna be boys there? Or are you actually meeting a girl?" Jaiden turned to his sister as she spoke and came into the kitchen. She leaned against the wall and folded her arms while giving him a look that said, *"I know what you're up to."* Abby was only a year younger than Jaiden but way more trouble.

"No, just the guys," he insisted. Jaiden tried to smile sweetly. "Mom always says to look nice."

His mom smiled liking that answer. She said, "Every time you leave this house you represent this family," she patted Jaiden's chest. "Besides, Jaiden does *not* have time for a girl. He's got to stay focused on school."

Good thing I lied, Jaiden thought.

Abby rolled her eyes and went back to the living room, bored that Jaiden wasn't getting in trouble.

"I got my test back today." He handed his dad the paper once he was sat at the table. He stood quietly as his parents looked at it, his mom observing from over his dad's shoulder.

"Good job," his dad said.

"So proud of you." After a kiss on the forehead, his mom continued working on dinner.

"So," Jaiden let his sentence hang.

"What boys?" his father questioned.

"Some guys from the team."

"Hm," was the only response.

"Coach is always talking about how we should not just be a team but be a family," Jaiden reasoned. He sat down next to his dad during the spiel. "And we have a big game coming up this weekend so we thought we would hang out." *This lie is getting out of control,* Jaiden stressed on the inside. His stomach was tied up in knots. He knew that if he got caught, his life was over. At least for a while.

"Alright," his dad sighed. "But be home by eight."

"Thank you, thank you!"

"But first," his mom interjected. "Let's eat."

JAIDEN'S FINGERS tapped anxiously on his phone while he sat on a bench waiting for Sofia. He tried distracting himself with social media or games but he couldn't help feeling guilty about lying. It might not have been the biggest lie a kid had ever told, but they were sure going to think so if they found out. Jaiden always did the right thing. He hated disappointing his parents. Especially when they already had Abby to deal with.

"Don't make everything we've done for you, end up being a waste!" his mother yelled as Abby cried.

Jaiden sat at the top of the stairs listening. He felt so bad for his sister but she got herself into the mess.

"It's not even a big deal!" Abby yelled back.

Jaiden shook his head. She should know better than to raise her voice back at her. Jaiden flinched when he heard his mother's hand connect with Abby's face.

"You do not raise your voice at me," their mom said shakily.

"You think your life is hard?" Jaiden shivered at his dad's chilly, calm tone."You should have lived through my childhood. You have it easy here and all we get is your complaining. Go to your room and do not come out until I say so."

Jaiden sighed at the memory. It had been a couple of months since that night, and Abby hadn't caused a scene since. He didn't know what she did to cause them to be so angry at her. She didn't want to talk about it after that night, and Jaiden couldn't blame her. A few days later, she had come to his room.

"It's not fair, J," Abby ranted. She walked around Jaiden's bedroom fidgeting with his books and trophies and other random stuff he had displayed on shelves.

"It's life," he replied matter of factly. "They're our parents. We have to obey them. They're just looking out for us." He felt the need to defend his parents even though he knew exactly how his sister felt. It wasn't fair that there was all this pressure. It wasn't fair that they felt like they could never make a mistake. But it's just the way it was.

"No wonder you're the favorite," she grumbled.

"They don't have favorites," Jaiden argued.

Abby stared at the baseball trophy, "I can't wait to get away from them."

Abby left Jaiden's room after she had said that. Her words echoed in his mind almost every day. He didn't doubt that she would leave one day and never come back. He felt anger rise up inside of him because it was like his parents didn't care or didn't notice. He felt guilty because he knew they focused on him more, but it's not like he asked for it.

It's not like he wanted it. Sometimes he just wanted to disappear.

Hands came over Jaidens eyes, and a familiar voice said, "Guess who?"

"Grandma?" Jaiden guessed. He smiled as Sofia let out a loud laugh. She walked around in front of him.

"Ha ha, very funny. You should be a comedian," she joked.

He stood up in front of her. "Yeah, my parents would love that."

They chuckled and then stood quiet for a minute. Both were too nervous to know what to say.

"Hey," Sofia smiled shyly.

"Hey," Jaiden said back. After a moment of hesitation, he hugged her.

"So, what's the plan?" she asked.

"Let's walk? Maybe get ice cream or something?" he suggested. *So corny, I should've planned better,* Jaiden mentally scolded himself.

"That sounds fun." Sofia seemed genuinely excited about it, to Jaiden's surprise.

They started walking through the park talking about school and teachers. Before he could convince himself not to, Jaiden reached out and held her hand. Sofia stopped talking for a second, caught off guard, but then squeezed his hand and continued.

"I failed the test miserably. I didn't study very well," Sofia said.

"What did your parents say?" Jaiden asked.

"They said to do better next time." She laughed and started talking about how her parents can't stand the education system most times.

My parents would have killed me, Jaiden thought. If he brought home anything less than a B, they would almost freeze him out. His dad would be so disappointed he would barely look at Jaiden. He would just have this angry face on for days. And all Jaiden would hear was, *'you can do better than that. You're just being lazy,'* or *'no one is going to do it for you. Opportunity doesn't just fall in your lap.'*

"Oh my gosh! The carousel! Can we go?" Sofia squealed.

Jaiden didn't even realize they had walked to this part of the park. Sometimes he would bring his youngest sister here so she could ride the carousel. The park glowed from its lights, and the whimsical music made it feel like they were in a movie.

"Yeah, of course," he told her. She smiled wide.

They stood in line, and he listened to her talk about her favorite show and the drama happening on it. All he could think about was where they were going to sit. Should it be a bench or on separate animals? If they sat on a bench, maybe he would try to kiss her. *That's romantic, right?*

They stepped onto the carousel, still holding hands.

"Bench? Or an animal?" Sofia asked.

"Whatever you want." Jaiden felt like that was the safest answer.

"Okay, bench it is." They sat down, and once everyone was on, the ride started spinning, and the music got louder.

Jaiden tried to calm himself down. He had never been this nervous for anything before. Sofia looked at him and smiled. They stared at each other for a second and Jaiden finally worked up his nerve. *Okay, this is it. Just lean in and kiss her. Easy.* He took a deep breath and they both started to lean in.

And then, Sofia disappeared.

3. LAURA

"Laura, are you packed? Let's go. I'm gonna be late!"

Laura sat on her bed staring at her shoes, ignoring her mom as she called from down the hallway. She gripped the blanket on her bed so tight it hurt her fingers. She just wanted to be alone, to sit in a room by herself until she felt better.

"Laura!" Her mom yelled again.

If she didn't respond soon, her bedroom door would be flung open and she'd get in trouble for being disrespectful. *I hate her,* she thought to herself.

"Lau-"

"Yeah!" she yelled, cutting her mom, Jessica, off.

"Let's go! Now!" Laura heard the front door open.

She groaned and stomped around her bedroom as she put her backpack on and picked up the bag that she had stuffed with clothes. Her mom was in the car waiting impatiently. Laura rolled her eyes, out of sight, of course. Otherwise, she would've gotten lectured the whole ride to her dad's.

"Now, I don't care if he says you can. You know what

shows you're not allowed to watch. And don't be staying up too late, you'll ruin your sleep schedule, and then next week will be a nightmare getting you up for school. And..."

Laura leaned her head against the window and ignored the next seventeen rules Jessica was giving her. Her mom always did this. She had to make sure it was known how bad of a father Laura's dad was. She had once heard her mom say on the phone that he was 'too much of a friend and not a parent.' *She's just jealous that I like him more,* Laura concluded.

This going back and forth between houses thing was fairly new. Her parents had only split up less than a year ago. Every other weekend Laura would stay with her dad. She counted down the days until she could go to his house. He was fun. He didn't constantly yell or give her a list of things not to do. They would watch movies, play games, and order take-out.

He bought her a phone, took her to the movies, and had even talked about taking her on vacation. 'He's so immature and irresponsible,' her mother had commented when Laura came home and told her all this. After hearing her parents have a screaming match on the phone about it, Laura stopped telling her mom anything that happened at her dad's. It wasn't worth the trouble.

The car slowed to a stop in front of the apartment. Laura wasted no time hopping out and grabbing her things. Her dad came out of the front door of the apartment building and smiled wide at her.

"Matt," Jessica said from inside the car. Matt looked at her, his smile dropping instantly. "Remember, she has that project to do this weekend. I really need it done here. It's due on Monday."

"Got it," he deadpanned. Laura stood beside him.

"And take it easy on the junk food and staying up late. It's throwing off her schedule," Jessica added.

Laura rolled her eyes.

"Got it," her dad said again with a bit more attitude.

"And—"

"Jessica," he interrupted, "how about next time, you write out a list of the do's and don'ts and pin it to her backpack. I've been a parent for 13 years, I think I've got it under control. We'll see you Sunday." He turned and started heading into the building.

Laura reluctantly went to the passenger window to say goodbye. Her mom's eyes looked glassy, like she wanted to cry.

"Mom?" Laura said, surprised at the expression on her mom's face.

Jessica immediately shook her head and forced a smile. She sighed, "I'll see you later, baby. I love you."

Laura nodded her head. "Love you too," she said softly.

She waved as her mom drove off and then followed her dad to the apartment. Sometimes Laura forgot that she still has her dad, but her mom doesn't. *She must be lonely.* Now, Laura felt guilty for giving her attitude, for thinking she hated her. *Ugh.*

Laura went to her room and put her clothes away. She hated packing and unpacking. She always ended up forgetting to bring stuff with her back and forth. The room at her mom's house was where she had grown up. She definitely liked it a lot better than the one at her dad's where the walls were white and empty. No pictures anywhere, no memories of their family.

"So, what are we doing tonight?" Laura asked her dad

excitedly as she walked into the living room and sat down next to him on the couch.

He typed away on his phone. She noticed he changed out of his t-shirt into a nice button-down shirt. He had even put on cologne.

"Are we going somewhere?" she wondered. He finally stopped texting and looked at her.

"I actually have to go out for a work thing. I'll be home late, so the place is yours tonight. Do you want me to order you pizza or Chinese?" He asked while looking at his phone again.

Disappointment hit Laura's heart. *He's just gonna leave? He hasn't seen me in a week and we only have a couple of days together to spend. Did he not care? Did he not miss me? Was he really a jerk and all those other names mom always called him? Was I being played? By my own dad?*

"So?" She realized he had been talking to her.

"What?"

"Pizza or Chinese?" he repeated.

"Chinese," she mumbled. He handed her his phone.

"Order real quick, and then I gotta go, okay?"

She took the phone from his hand, and he went into his room. She called the restaurant and ordered extra food just to make him mad when he saw the bill. *He deserves it.* She hung up and looked up at his bedroom door—he was still in there.

Quickly she went to his messages and saw the most recent conversation was with a girl named Victoria. She read through the messages quickly so she wouldn't get caught. *He's a liar. He wasn't going to a work thing. He was going on a date.* She felt her face getting hot with anger. *He'd rather be with her than me.* She quickly locked his phone and set it on the couch.

"Done?" he asked after he had come out of his room. She nodded her head, barely looking at him. "I'll see you later. Don't stay up too late, don't watch anything you're not supposed to, and if you need anything, just text me. Okay?" He kissed her on the forehead. "Love ya."

"Love ya," she muttered. He waved goodbye, and she locked the door after he left.

She wiped her eyes and tried to stop more tears from falling. She wanted her mom. She wanted to go back home. This wasn't home. This was his new life. He had a new girlfriend, and someday he'd have new kids. More tears fell at that thought. He was going to have a whole new family. Where was she going to fit into that?

Her sadness quickly turned to anger when she thought about her mom. She was sad and tired all the time because she had to work extra shifts, and here her dad was going out like a teenager. *What a jerk.*

THE FOOD ARRIVED, and Laura stuffed her face and watched TV. Even her favorite show wasn't making her laugh. She was so upset. So hurt. *Parents suck,* she thought. She looked at her phone. It was still early in the evening.

Before she could talk herself out of it, she left the apartment. Her dad had said he wouldn't be home 'till late, so it's not like he'd even know. She went out one of the side doors of the building so the doorman wouldn't see her.

She had never snuck out before, but drastic times call for drastic measures. She put her headphones in and walked to the park. She listened to her music loudly and texted her friend group chat about what had happened.

She had told them to meet her at the park to hang out. They agreed, but it'd be a little while before they could get there. She needed something to do in the meantime.

She turned her music up louder and scrolled through her social media. She didn't double-tap most of the pictures she saw. She didn't want to give those people that satisfaction. *Their life is so amazing? Good for them. No one cared.* Except, she did care. She wanted that kind of life. She wanted the life she had months ago before her parents ruined everything.

Just because they were unhappy didn't mean they had to make her unhappy with them. They were so selfish. *I wish I had different parents.* She imagined a different life with a mom and dad who were happy and in love. She even imagined some siblings. A different life that wasn't so lonely. *That'd be nice.*

She closed her apps, annoyed at the world, and put her phone in her pocket. As she walked through the park she saw bright lights flashing through the trees a little ways ahead. She followed the lights and they continued to get brighter. She saw a carousel spinning. *Might as well.*

She got in line as the ride came to a stop. The gate opened and the people in front of her started to move. She saw a shiny tiger, climbed on, strapped herself in, and off she went.

4. ELIJAH

"Mom, I swear I really am sick." Elijah coughed again and pulled his blanket tighter around his shoulders. He sat in the kitchen as his mom made her morning coffee. The sun came in through the windows, warming up the room even though the floor tiles still felt like ice. "I don't feel good at all."

"Well, you made quite an effort to walk all the way down here and tell me that." Vanessa faced her son with a hand on her hip. She tilted her head and wore a small smile as she waited to hear his explanation.

"Mom, the flu has been going around. You got the e-mail from the school!" Elijah spoke with his hands. "If my immune system, as weak as it is right now, gets around people who carry the flu virus, then I'm done for!"

Vanessa rolled her eyes and sighed. She turned around, poured coffee into her thermos, wiped the counter clean, and then turned to face her son again with an eyebrow raised.

"This is the second time this week you've tried to stay home. And a couple of weeks ago, you had 'headaches.'" She did dramatic air quotes and emphasized the word headaches. "What's going on? Is there a test today? Did you not do your homework?"

Elijah almost wished his mom had asked him if someone was bothering him at school. That way, him admitting it wouldn't be as pathetic. But no, his mom couldn't imagine him getting beat up by anyone.

"Yeah." Elijah hung his head to make the lie believable. "I was supposed to do two pages of math, and I didn't even start."

"You made that choice. You deal with the consequences. You need to take responsibility with your teacher. Go get dressed. I'll be in the car." She put her purse over her shoulder and walked out the front door.

Elijah let out a frustrated groan and sulked to his room. *Dad would have let me stay home,* he thought to himself. As he got dressed, his mind raced, trying to come up with a plan to survive the day without receiving the beating Adam "owed" him.

He wouldn't be anywhere without other people around, he would be the last to leave every class, and he would eat lunch in the nurse's office. He'd just tell her his head was hurting again. Then, he would wait in the library until the school was practically empty. *Maybe mom could pick me up today.*

"I'm sorry, sweetie, I can't. I have a house to show. You'll have to walk." Vanessa responded as she backed out of their driveway. Elijah had crossed his fingers when he asked her to pick him up, but of course, it was just his luck that she couldn't. He leaned his head against the window. *You'll be fine. Just stick to the plan.*

Elijah followed his plan step by step as soon as he was

dropped off. The morning, thankfully, had been uneventful (besides Elijah getting a lecture from his math teacher since he really hadn't done the homework). He had seen Adam a couple of times walking down the hall, but they hadn't run into each other. The only classes they were in together were art and gym, and today they had neither.

"Hey, Elijah."

Elijah stopped walking down the hallway and turned to see his history teacher standing in the doorway to his classroom. He smiled, raising his gray mustache.

"Hey, Mr. B."

"Where you headed? Lunch room is that way." He used his thumb to point down the hall to the loud cafeteria—the battleground Elijah was avoiding at all costs.

It's not like he had any friends to sit with and shield him, so being there was like walking into a trap. He could already imagine everyone laughing as Adam knocked his food out of his hands and launched insults at him.

"Yeah, my head kinda hurts so I'm going to see the nurse," Elijah explained.

Mr. B nodded. "You do that often, huh? I usually see you walking by around this time."

"Yeah," Elijah drew out the word, having no idea what to say next. *Please let me go. Please don't make me sit in the cafeteria,* he begged silently.

"Would you like to eat lunch with me? We can sit right here in the hallway."

"Um–" Elijah tried to think of an excuse.

"C'mon, I promise it will be more exciting than Mrs. Davis' room. And it won't smell like a Clorox dump," Mr. B smiled.

Elijah chucked. *Guess it won't be that bad.* "Okay," he told him.

"Great! I'll be right back," Mr. B said before walking back into his classroom.

Elijah slid down the wall and sat crossed-legged. He opened his lunch and looked over what his mom had packed. Mr. B came back out of his classroom with a thermos and a spoon.

"My wife makes the best chili." He took a couple of bites, and Elijah unwrapped his sandwich. "How's your mom doing?" Mr. B asked after a moment.

"She's good," he answered robotically.

It was the same question everyone always asked, and Elijah always gave the same response. He knew the next thing Mr. B would say before he did it, and he had his answer ready.

"And how are you?" *Yep, classic.*

"I'm good." Elijah took a bite of his sandwich. *I should probably start on that English project when I get home. I should have told mom to buy the stuff I need.*

"My dad died too, when I was ten." Elijah looked up, caught completely off guard. Mr. B continued softly, "Everything felt different afterward. The house felt empty. I felt alone and angry. And, like you, I mastered the art of giving fake answers convincingly so people would stop talking to me. I know how it feels."

Elijah averted his eyes. He was not expecting to have this kind of conversation today or ever. He responded quietly, unsure of responding at all, "It's hard for my mom to talk about it. So, we don't."

He had been to therapy a couple of times, but it hadn't helped him feel any better. It was like his mom was making him go because everyone told her it was the right thing to do. All he wanted, though, was to talk to her, not a stranger.

"Yeah, my mom was the same way, but talking can help. It's just hard for some people to voice how they feel."

"Thanks." Elijah couldn't even look up at Mr. B. If he did, he would definitely cry like a baby right there in the hall. That was the last thing he wanted anyone to see.

"I felt like I had to be strong for my mom since my dad couldn't anymore." Mr. B took another bite of chili.

"That's how I feel." Elijah peeled the crust off his sandwich as he confessed what he hadn't told anyone. "I don't want to add more stress or problems or anything, so I tell her everything's good."

After a moment, Mr. B asked, "But it's not?"

Elijah remembered two weeks ago when Adam had cornered him in the bathroom and punched him in the stomach a few times. If he told Mr. B about it, Elijah would be considered a snitch, and Adam would make him pay.

"I mean, life's not perfect, you know?" Elijah shrugged and put the rest of his sandwich in his mouth.

"Oh, I know." Mr. B smiled.

They ate in silence for a few minutes. Elijah couldn't help but think of his dad, even though he kept trying to distract himself from doing it.

"How did he die? Your dad?" Elijah asked, then immediately regretted it. "I'm sorry, I, I, shouldn't have asked that."

"No, it's okay." Mr. B reassured him. "He was really sick, had been for as long as I could remember. He died in his sleep one night."

Before Elijah could think about what he was saying, he started talking, "My dad was in a car crash. A truck hit him.

He was in the hospital for a day before he died. He was on his way home from work."

"I'm so sorry," Mr. B spoke softly.

"Yeah." The harsh ringing of the bell drowned out Elijah's small voice.

"If you ever want to talk about it, I'm here," Mr. B offered as they packed up their lunches.

"Thanks." Elijah smiled and, for the first time in a long time, really meant it.

Elijah's knee bounced up and down as he sat in the back corner of the library. It was almost five o'clock. He could probably head home and avoid Adam if Adam didn't end up staying at school for some reason. The two of them had a brief encounter in the hallway after lunch. Adam just gave a look that pretty much promised trouble.

Elijah put his books in his backpack and picked up his empty candy wrappers. On the plus side, he finished his homework and the work that he was late on. He was an okay student but had had trouble focussing lately. His mom and the therapist told the school it was because of his grief. He didn't know how much he agreed with that. He just didn't care about school. He had bigger things to worry about, like not getting beat up every day.

He walked out of the school building and looked around to make sure he didn't see any of his regular bullies. There was a group of kids that followed Adam everywhere. They always hyped him up when he was being a jerk. *I wish I had a personal cheerleading team,* Elijah chuckled to himself.

As he left the school property and started home, he let

out a sigh of relief. His plan today had worked. Now he just had to get through tomorrow. And the next day. And the next day. He groaned and felt his chest start to tighten.

"I am calm. I am relaxed. I am calm. I am relaxed," Elijah mumbled under his breath, over and over, the mantra his therapist begged him to try. She suggested he repeat it to himself when he starts to feel angry, or anxious, or any unknown emotion. Sometimes it worked but most times, it didn't.

He got angry so easily lately. He was always embarrassed about it, but he couldn't help it. When it happened, he felt like he was going to explode. He wished he would explode and fight back when Adam was bothering him, but he was always too scared. Instead of getting angry when Adam was around, he would get super anxious and quiet.

He kicked a rock and watched it fly forward on the sidewalk. "I am calm. I am relaxed. I am calm, I am–" *Dead,* he said to himself. There was Adam and his friends standing on the corner a block ahead of him. He would have to pass them to get home unless he cut through the park. It would take longer, but it would be a lot less painful.

He started to turn to the left when he heard one of Adam's friends say his name. He didn't have to look to know that they had seen him. He took off running. He could hear them shouting and laughing behind him as he ran as fast as his feet could take him. The park sat in the middle of their town, and it was huge. It had a couple of bridges, a playground, a basketball court and lots of trees. *I could climb one, and they wouldn't think to look there.*

Elijah took a sharp right turn and saw a perfect tree for climbing. He grabbed onto a low branch and started to ascend, but he wasn't going as fast as he had hoped. He could hear the boys behind him. *Tree climbing, bad idea.*

He hopped down and started running again. *A crowd. Look for a crowd.* He heard people chattering up ahead of him, so he kept sprinting in that direction. Music hit his ears as he ran into a clearing in the park. *The carousel!* Elijah had forgotten all about it. He could hide there in a seat. No way would Adam get on it to look for him.

He stood in the line, ducking behind people and ignoring the looks they were giving him. He could see Adam scanning the crowd. Elijah stepped onto the carousel and found a bench to duck down into. He took a deep breath and got comfortable.

He could be here for a while.

5. TROUBLE

"Ladies and gentlemen," the ringleader's voice filled the Big Top, but he could not be seen. "Boys and girls." Colorful lights darted across the excited audience. "Children of all ages." The children bounced up and down with cotton candy in hand. "Tonight, we will steal you away from your world. We will invade your mind, your heart, and your dreams. Miracles will materialize right before your very eyes."

"Here at this circus, we believe that the impossible is possible!" his voice got louder, filled with excitement, "there is no such thing as ordinary, no such thing as average! Tonight you will experience freedom! Freedom from human logic. Freedom from what you think you know. You are entering a place from which you will never wish to leave!"

The quiet music that had been playing behind him got louder and more intense. Massive colorful posters of various circus acts hung from the top of the tent, slightly swaying back and forth. Bleachers holding thousands of people were arranged in a circle, with the band settled in an orchestra pit.

27

"It is my pleasure and my privilege." The lights went red and expanded across the audience in the stands. "To welcome you all." The crowd went wild. "To Cirque." The drums echoed. "Des." Smoke began to rise from the ground of the circus ring. "Élus," the ringleader bellowed as the band played. Lights flashed every color imaginable, and the audience stood to their feet cheering.

A navy blue curtain, covered with sparkling silver stars, opened for the ringleader to enter through it. He was riding a larger-than-life gold unicycle. He wore a dark blue pea coat, a black top hat, and a huge smile. The lights reflected off of the swirls of gold on his coat. He rode around waving to the audience and encouraging the musicians to play louder.

"Greetings and salutations! I am the ringleader here at Cirque Des Élus!" Sparkling fireworks went off all around the audience. The response was happy screams and clapping. "We have quite a show for you tonight. So sit tight and open your mind," he spoke excitedly, gesturing with his hands and widening his eyes. "To kick off our adventure, take a deep breath and feast your eyes on the sky!" He raised his right hand and his head straight up, and all the lights went black except for the ceiling of the Big Top Tent, which was illuminated with white light.

On the right side of the tent, six people stood tall on platforms wearing full-body navy blue leotards. The women had their hair pulled up, and the silver sequins that adorned their costume glimmered in the spotlight. The men had silver stripes running up the sides of their costumes.

"Today, you will see these brave, talented performers swing from bar-to-bar, person-to-person, limb-to-limb, at an unbelievable fifty feet in the air! Here they are, the highly regarded Masters of the Trapeze!" the ringleader's voice bellowed from the darkness, and all attention was focused solely upward.

Two bars hung from the ceiling, one on the left, one on the right. A Trapeze Artist was lowered between them, hanging upside down with the backs of his knees resting on the bar. He began swinging back and forth. Another performer stood at the edge of the lowest of the two platforms on the left side, awaiting the perfect moment to leap forward. The audience gasped as she threw herself into the air and grabbed ahold of his hands. They swung back and forth. Every so often she would let go of him and flip to grab onto another bar that had been lowered. There was a pit in every audience member's stomach as they watched.

More trapeze bars were lowered from the ceiling, and the Trapeze Artists jumped into the act. They went back and forth, swinging off of one another, doing flips, and adding more people to their count until all eight people were soaring above the audience.

The spotlight above shut off as deep intense drumming again flowed from the band. A dozen men and women dressed in all black marched to the middle of the ring and stood shoulder to shoulder in a circle. A dark red light covered them. In the middle of the group was a giant black fire pit that they had rolled out with them. The Fire Breathers all bowed their heads and as soon as they did, a fire erupted in the middle of the pit.

Their boots shook the ground as they stomped along with the drums. There were specks of orange and red in their black clothing that could only be seen when the light moved across them a certain way. Their hair was gelled back and a curved design was painted on both sides of their faces, from their foreheads to their chins.

A light shone on the ringleader as he stood on an elevated platform in the middle of the orchestra pit. His voice was deep and serious, "And now, arguably the most dangerous force of nature will be thrown, touched, swallowed, and controlled. With no protection between them and the flame, I present, the Fire Breathers." The light went off of him, and the Fire Breathers again became the focus of attention.

In their left hands was a black torch. They all turned and walked in sync to the pit and lit the torches. They then turned back around and walked a few feet away from the pit, and tossed the torch to their right hand. Then they increased the pace. Left, then right, then left, then right, then back and forth between performers.

Every Fire Breather pulled out another torch. Holding both sticks in their left hand, they took their right-hand pointer finger and thumb and reached into the flame. They held the fire between their fingers and carried it to the other torch, and lit it. The crowd applauded, not thinking it could get any more insane. The Fire Breathers twirled their torches around and caused an uproar when they swiped the fire across their tongues.

"No way!" Someone shouted while watching with eyes and mouth wide open.

The Fire Breathers put a torch into their mouth and held onto the burning end with their teeth. They took the torch out and did it again with the other one. They then went back and forth with their torches breathing on each and expanding the flame far out in front of them. There was wild applause and cheers when the fire subsided, and the lights came back on. The group took their bows, and left marching to the drums.

"That was unbelievable!" several people shouted.

"From the plains of India, we present the Mighty Brutus, the Lovely Evangeline, and the Precious Marco." Upbeat music and three elephants followed the ringleader's introduction. They all wore colorful jewels and clothes, as did the people standing on top of their backs doing all sorts of tricks while keeping their balance. The child that stood on Marco did a handstand while the baby elephant held Evangeline's tail as they followed behind Brutus. After making a full circle, the majestic creatures lined up and stood on their hind legs.

They each took a turn blowing their nature-given trumpet. Brutus' was deep and assertive, followed by the strong cry of Evangeline. Precious Marco was nothing compared to his parents, but it made no difference. His tiny trunk drew "aw's" from the audience and left the children begging for an elephant as a pet.

The elephant trainers did a flip off of the elephants back and brought in yellow and white performance balls in different sizes. Each trainer whistled for their elephant, and the elephants stepped forward and put one leg at a time on the ball until they were standing on it. Brutus started rolling first. Evangeline followed, and Marco rolled on after them. They went around the circus ring three times, following their trainers' commands. Then all three came to a stop and gave out a loud trumpet one last time.

"Now," The ringleader stood in the middle of the arena. "Lift your eyes once more! Balancing on a wire so thin they might as well be treading on air, 60 feet above the ground, the Tightrope Walkers!"

The top of the circus tent was illuminated once again as two people faced each other. One on the right side of a long rope and one on the left. They wore white bodysuits with a dark purple cursive C on their backs and white slippers. The music began as the first step was taken.

"What happens if they fall?" a worried wife asked her husband as she gripped his arm tightly.

The rope walkers' arms were stretched horizontally to keep their balance. As the pair got closer to each other, the crowd began to whisper and murmur questions about how they would pass each other on the rope. The music paused as the walkers met each other in the middle. The walker on the right grabbed the waist of their companion, lifted them up, and spun them around to the other side, allowing them to continue their cross to the platforms. The crowd cheered, some of their uneasiness diminishing.

Suddenly though, as each tightrope walker began towards the platforms, the circus tent began to shake. The rope walker's smiles fell, and they bent their knees more to keep their balance. A rumbling sound echoed along with the voices of the worried audience.

"What's going on?" one woman questioned.

"They're gonna fall!" a child shouted and pointed up at the circus performers high in the air doing their best to stay standing.

A rush of warm wind blew into the tent like a hurricane, and both walkers let out a scream as they fell. The whole circus, performers and audience members alike, were on their feet and yelling. No one knew what to do in the middle of this chaos. Everyone watching breathed a sigh of relief when the tightrope walkers landed in the net. They each bounced up and down a few times but they gave a thumbs up to let their ringleader know they were fine.

Just as quickly as it started, the shaking ceased. The ringleader now stood on the platform in the middle of the orchestra pit. He raised his arms and began to talk to his frenzied audience. The spotlight illuminated him.

"Ladies and gentlemen, boys and girls, all is well." He smiled. The crowd stopped talking and listened closely to the man in the top hat. "For the safety of all of you and the performers of Cirque, we are going to end the show here. Please safely make your way to the exits and be sure to come again. Thank you for spending your evening with us." The ringleader's calm demeanor put the audience at ease.

People clamored to leave. They all released a scream at the sudden darkness. Barnaby raced to get the lights back on. The ringleader didn't move. A furious expression replaced his peaceful smile. A black shadow figure with no face appeared in front of him. The ringleader didn't say a word. He clenched his jaw and his fists.

The shadow figure began to laugh. The laugh was deep and sounded like out-of-tune music. As the shadow laughed, more figures appeared behind it, all cackling too. It was a horrible sound. Everyone in the circus tent covered their ears and winced. Everyone but the ringleader.

"Enough," he demanded.

The Shadows silenced immediately. They couldn't help but obey the power that the ringleader emanated.

"Ladies and gentlemen," the Shadow began to mock. "Boys and girls–"

"You have no business here. Leave," the ringleader interrupted.

"My influence is growing in the world, *ringleader,*" the

Shadow spat his title. "The greater my power grows there, the greater it grows here. Soon, I will just have to let out a single breath, and your circus will come crumbling down to nothing. As it should be."

"Impossible." The ringleader was calmer now. The tension left his shoulders, and he casually put his hands in his pockets. He would show no emotion to these vile creatures. "My circus will *never* crumble."

"Just wait and watch, *ringleader*," the shadow said with distaste.

The lights came back on, and the dark army of shadows was gone. The tent was empty of the audience now. The performers had gotten everyone safely out. There was a hush all around. The performers were too shocked to move or speak.

"R.L.?" Barnaby addressed the ringleader.

"How did they manage all of that?" R.L. asked, still looking at where the shadows had been.

"I, I don't know," Barnaby hung his head. "I will make sure the people of Ekklesia know there is no threat to them."

"Thank you," R.L. said as he stepped down from the platform. He put a hand on his friend's shoulder comfortingly. R.L. turned to see the tightrope walkers that had fallen. "Milo, Mia are you alright?" he asked them.

"Yes," Mia nodded. "Just shaken up, but we're alright." Milo, her brother, nodded in agreement.

6. ADAM

dam rubbed his shoulder as he sat on the school bus. *'You idiot!'* He flinched as he remembered the fight he had with his mom that morning and the words she had yelled. He looked around to make sure no one noticed his reaction. He hadn't meant to make his mom angry. She was just always mad, making it unfortunately easy to set her off.

He had tripped, hit his shoulder on the wall, and dropped his phone down the stairs causing it to shatter. His mom was furious, *'I don't have the money to buy you a new one. So now, you don't get one. Hope you don't get into trouble 'cause you got no way to call for help.'* She had smacked him on the back of the head.

He stared out of the dirty window of the bus, mad that now he couldn't even listen to music. Instead, he had to listen to these dumb kids talking all around him. These dumb, lucky kids. He glanced at his peers quickly, his fists clenching in anger. They laughed with their phones and nice headphones and clothes and sneakers.

He tucked his feet under the worn leather seat out of habit. *Maybe no one will notice.* His mom got his sneakers second-hand, from other people and stores that just sold junk. *'Clothes and shoes aren't important. Having the lights on in the house and food to eat is.'* He pulled some foam from the already cut open bus seat.

Adam had already decided he wasn't going home straight after school today. His mom wouldn't notice anyway. She was always working late. She didn't want to be home with him any more than he wanted to be home with her. He couldn't wait till he turned eighteen. He'd leave her and never ever look back.

The bus made a screeching noise as it pulled up to the school. Adam grabbed his backpack and pushed through the other kids to get off. He met up with a couple of his buddies, Anthony and Isaac, in homeroom. He doodled in his notebook until the bell rang. He was always drawing hurricanes, just ovals in black ink over and over and over.

When the bell rang for first period, Adam and his friends bumped shoulders with everyone they could on the way to English class. They laughed at the looks they got.

"You guys wanna hang this weekend?" Anthony asked the boys.

"Yeah!" Issac said enthusiastically.

"Um," Adam spoke. "Nah, I don't think I can." *'And you know what else? Since you're so irresponsible, you're grounded too. No hanging out until I say so. There's consequences for your actions.'* He knew better than to argue with his mom, even though he wanted nothing more than to scream at her the way she screamed at him.

"Why not?" Anthony pressed.

They entered their English class and sat down at their desks. All in the back row.

"I, uh, I," Adam tried to think of what to tell them that wouldn't be as embarrassing as being grounded. "Fine, but you can't tell anyone." The boys leaned in to hear Adam's secret. "I got a date."

Their eyes widened.

"No way," Isaac gawked.

Adam smiled and nodded.

"With who?" Anthony yelled in a hushed tone.

"Can't tell ya," Adam shrugged. His friends kept on bothering him for the name. He smiled. This was much better attention than knowing he was being punished. "Okay, okay," Adam relented. "I can't tell you her name, but I can tell you she's really hot."

The boys laughed and patted him on the back. They were jealous, jealous of his life. He has a good life. *I have a good life,* he tried to convince himself.

THE REST of the day passed like normal. Teachers being teachers, he and his friends making jokes and pestering their classmates. Adam just couldn't wait for the day to be over. He wanted to go to get food. He reached into his pocket and pulled out a few dollars. It was only enough for a soda and some chips. His stomach growled. The school lunch sucked and never filled him up.

He walked down the hallway after lunch, heading to his next period, and he spotted the person he hated almost as much as his mom.

"Hey, Eli," Adam dragged out his name. Elijah stared at him, not saying anything. He looked too scared to talk. Adam smirked at that. "See you around," he taunted and bumped his shoulder as he passed.

Adam sat in class and planned how he would corner Elijah after school and take his cash. He sure didn't need it. He had way more money than Adam did. He could just get more from his mom. Elijah had the perfect life. A perfect house, perfect money, and a nice perfect mom.

I wish you would be more like that Elijah kid, Adam's mother had told him on the way home from a parent-teacher conference last year.

Elijah had been the student of the month, so his picture was on the wall. Adam's mom had sarcastically asked when his picture would be on that wall. And to make matters worse, they had seen Elijah and his parents while they were at the school. They were all smiling and soft-spoken, and the teachers were all over them. Because of stupid Elijah, Adam had to listen to how much of a disappointment he was all the way home. He decided then that he hated him.

"Pass your homework forward," the teacher instructed.

Adam tore a page out of his notebook, with only his name written on the top, and passed it to the person sitting in front of him. The kid looked back at him, confused.

"What?" Adam snapped. The kid turned around quickly and passed the paper forward.

His teacher sifted through the work to check, and he stopped when he saw Adam's paper. Adam stared, waiting for the reaction. *He's probably gonna get sent to the principal's. He always did.* His teacher walked towards him holding the assignment.

"What is this?" Mr. Wilson put the blank page on Adam's desk.

"The homework," Adam deadpanned.

"Funny," Mr. Wilson's mouth was set in a firm line.

"Thanks," he smirked.

"Why wasn't this assignment completed?"

Adam shrugged, but he knew exactly why it wasn't completed.

"Adam! Adam come help me clean this house up!"

He was sitting in his room when his mom called for him. He had his book and notebook in front of him. He was planning to actually try with this assignment. He kind of liked what they were learning. History was interesting.

"I'm doing my homework!" Adam yelled back. He wrote his name on the top of the page.

"Excuse me?" His mom opened his bedroom door angrily. He turned around to face her.

"I'm doing homework," he said quietly.

"You can finish it after. You should have done it already. You've been home for hours. Come help me, now. You need to clean up your mess." She walked away, not waiting for him to say anything.

He looked at the clock. He had barely been home that long. And he wanted to relax after school before homework. He sighed and went to help his mom. By the time he was finished cleaning the house, with barely any help from her because apparently she was tired, he was too angry to think, so he just listened to music and fell asleep.

"If you won't take my class seriously you don't need to attend it today. Go to the principal." Mr. Wilson turned away.

Adam picked up his bag. He was used to this. Adults just thought they knew everything. They assumed kids were stupid and just there to be told what to do. They never considered that maybe life sucked for them too. But no, only being an adult was difficult. He slammed the classroom door behind him as he left.

He took his sweet time walking to the front office. They were just gonna make him sit there until the next period. No one was going to pay him any attention. He was just a problem they all ignored.

ADAM, Isaac, and Anthony all stood on the corner talking about girls they thought were hot. Adam peered over their shoulders as they looked up girls on social media. He had told them how he broke his phone and his new one was in the mail. He was gonna have to come up with another lie to explain why he wouldn't have a phone for a while.

"Adam, look, it's that Elijah kid." Isaac pointed across the street where Elijah was now running into the park.

"Let's go!" Adam shouted.

They took off after him. Adam had to admit, Elijah was fast. They followed him through the park and lost him for a minute. They turned and saw him trying to climb up a tree. The boys laughed as Elijah jumped down and continued running ahead.

He got too far ahead of them and they lost him in a crowd. People were all around and the music from the carousel was annoyingly loud. Adam pushed through people, not caring about what they said to him. Isaac and Anthony came up beside him.

"Lost him," Anthony sighed.

"He's around here somewhere." Adam kept walking through the crowd.

"Let's just go. We'll see him tomorrow," Isaac said.

"No," Adam argued. He wanted Elijah's cash and the satisfaction of scaring him.

"Adam, we're out," Isaac told him.

Adam shrugged his shoulders to his friends, "Whatever." It's not like Adam had anywhere else to go.

The two boys walked off, leaving him to continue the search. He walked around in circles for a while. He had no idea what time it was, but the sky was starting to get dark. Light blue was turning to navy blue, but he was still on a mission to find Elijah. He got more and more pissed the longer it took to find him. He stood still for a minute and watched the carousel go by.

He laughed aloud when he saw Elijah on his phone sitting on one of the benches. *Idiot.* The carousel stopped, and he waited to see if he would get off. When Elijah made no effort to leave, Adam pushed through the people getting on, and he walked right up to him.

"Hey," he said and laughed when Elijah's eyes widened.

The carousel started to move and Adam sat down. There was nowhere for either of the boys to go until this stupid thing stopped moving.

One of them gulped and one of them smiled.

7. STELLA

S tella sat on the carousel with her two younger cousins, Amy and Rob. They laughed and talked to each other as they went round and round. The little kids convinced Stella to let them ride for a second time, and she had a feeling there would be a third and fourth too.

She sighed and looked at her phone. No texts, no notifications. It was as dry as a desert. *It's pretty sad when the most frequent person on your text and call list is your grandma,* she thought to herself. She loved her grandma of course, but hated how she always got roped into babysitting.

Stella's mom and Amy and Rob's mom were sisters. She babysat the kids a lot since their mom worked the late shift at the hospital and their grandma worked a couple of nights a week. *It's what you do for family,* grandma would say. She didn't get paid for it, but every once in a while, her aunt would slip her a ten, and on a really good day a twenty. Tonight, her grandma wasn't working. Instead, Stella was on this stupid carousel for an entirely different reason.

"Stella," Amy got her attention. "Why didn't you want to talk to your mom?"

She knew one of the kids was gonna ask her about what happened earlier at the house, but she had been praying they'd forgotten. She had no idea what to say in response. She really wanted to pretend it was just another day, but there was no avoiding the situation.

❖

Stella had been watching a video on her phone while laying on the couch. Amy and Rob were watching TV, and their grandma was making dinner. A knock at the door stole Stella's attention away from the video. When another knock came and her grandma continued cooking, Stella figured she needed to answer it.

If she could've gone back in time and not opened the door, she would have. Standing in front of her was a woman that looked like Stella's own reflection, just with more years. She momentarily stopped breathing and her mind went blank.

"Stella," her mother said calmly. Stella hadn't seen or heard from her in a year. It hadn't been the first time she had dropped off the face of the earth, but it was the longest she had stayed gone. "Stella?" her mother repeated.

What am I supposed to say? Stella thought. The only thing she could think of was, 'I hate you.' But that probably wouldn't be the best option. "Grandma," she called out instead.

The small smile left her mom's face. They continued to stare at each other. Her mom looked skinnier, a lot skinnier. Her clothes were too big for her and her hair was longer. Stella noticed the gym bag that was sitting at her mom's feet. Probably filled with clothes. Oh no, Stella thought, she's gonna ask if she can stay here.

Just then, her grandma came to the door and told Stella to go to the living room. She had no emotion in her voice. Stella could hear the beginning of their conversation, each of them saying hello. And then the front door closed, cutting off the conversation from prying ears.

A few minutes later, they had come back in, and her mother walked into the kitchen. She said hello to Amy and Rob, but they hardly recognized her. She told them she was Stella's mom and they said hi with innocent smiles.

"Take them to the park. Here's some cash. Play, ride the carousel, stay out till I call you." Her grandmother put a few bills in her hands and started to get the kids ready to go outside.

"But–" Stella started to protest, but she got cut off.

"Get Robby's shoes on." Stella did as she was told. Her grandma offered no explanation, no words. She just rushed her three grandkids out the door.

AND NOW I'M on this stupid carousel, Stella huffed as she remembered. She was old enough to have stayed and heard the conversation. She was old enough to deserve a real reason why her mother had been gone for so long and why she decided to show up now.

"Stella, Stella, Stella." Amy pushed on her arm annoyingly.

"Stop it," she grumbled and jerked her arm away.

"Why didn't you wanna see your mom?" the little girl insisted.

"I did, but grandma wanted us to leave."

"Why?" Rob wondered.

Stella shrugged her shoulders.

`"Where has your mom been?" Amy asked.

Stella shrugged again. "She's been gone a long time." Couldn't even show up for my birthday.

She crossed her arms and stared hard at the dirty floor of the carousel they were on. *Was this thing ever gonna stop?* The kids began talking to each other again, leaving Stella to her thoughts.

She had only met her dad a couple of times before he moved to another city. Her mom had been around more but never consistently. She would leave and then come back when she needed something from Stella's grandma. Sometimes it was hard to believe that she was her mom's mom. They were so different.

Her grandma was always there. She had been taking care of Stella for as long as Stella could remember. She bought her clothes, fed her, went to school events when she needed to. She signed permission slips and punished her. She was more of her mom than her mother was.

Stella's face burned with anger. She knew her mom was at their house right now asking for money. Didn't she know that grandma was struggling with money too? She was working hard to raise Stella and help out her other kids when they needed it. She made a mental note not to ask for anything new for a while. She didn't want to add stress.

Pulling out her phone, she sent a text asking if they could come home now. She wanted to talk to her mom before she left again. Who knows when, or if, she would ever be back. Stella had some questions for her. *Where have you been? Why didn't you visit? Why are you so skinny? Why don't you want me?*

That last question hit her hard. It made her heart hurt and her eyes burn as they filled up with tears. It's a question she asked in her mind a lot but had never said out loud. *Why didn't her mom want her? Why didn't she stay to take care of her? Why didn't she care enough to at least visit?*

"Can we ride again after this?" Rob begged. Amy whined in agreement.

"No, we're gonna go home." She was determined to see her mom even if her grandma didn't want her to. The kids groaned and kept persisting. Just then, her phone started buzzing. She looked at the name of who was calling and answered right away. "Hey," she said.

"You can bring the kids back. Dinner's ready," her grandma's voice was normal like it had been just a regular night.

"What happened? Is she still there?" Stella asked quickly.

"No."

"What? Where did she go? Why did you make her leave? I wanted to talk to her." Stella couldn't help the attitude in her voice.

"She needed to leave. She's not in a good place. You don't need to talk to her when she's like that."

"How could you do that? That's not fair!" She didn't care that her voice was getting louder. She didn't even notice her cousins had stopped playing and just stared at her.

"Don't argue with me, Stella!" her grandma yelled back. "Come home. Now." The call ended, and Stella just stared at the phone. Her heart was beating so fast, and her throat was tightening up.

"Stella?" Amy asked quietly. She was a smart little girl and knew better than to mess with her older cousin right now.

The carousel came to a screeching stop. People started to get off as a new crowd boarded. Stella inhaled deeply and didn't move.

"We're riding again," she told the kids. They nodded and started whispering to each other.

There was no way Stella was going home right now. She

was way too angry. She knew she would yell at her grandma and get herself into so much trouble. *How could she?* Stella had a right to talk to her mom. What did she mean she wasn't in a good place? She looked fine, sort of.

She took deep breaths. She would go home and be nice and then she would be on a mission to find her mom. She would look through her grandma's phone, ask her aunts and uncles. She would search the streets and hospitals if she had to. Either way, Stella was going to talk to her mom and get some answers.

"We're going home after this ride," Stella said while chipping the nail polish off of her thumb. She didn't get a reply from either of the kids, which was weird. They always had something to say.

"Hey, I said–" Stella gasped at the empty seat next to her. "No, no, no," she said as she stood up and scanned the area frantically. The more she looked around, the more freaked out she got. The once crowded carousel was quiet except for the music that continued to play.

Everyone was gone.

8. CAROUSEL

The lights—red, blue, yellow—flashed as the carousel spun. The mechanical music seemed to be getting louder and louder with each turn. Red, blue, yellow. The horses, the tigers, and bears rose up and down. Up and down. Children's giggles and adult's laughter were muffled under the tune that bounced off the gold poles.

Red, blue, yellow. Red, blue, yellow. The colors all smeared together. Red, blue, yellow. Red, blue, yellow.

Then, the colors started to slow down, and the music too. Slower, and slower and s l o w e r.

Until the carousel finally came to a stop.

"Hello?" Jaiden said as he stood up, panicking. *Where the heck is Sophia? Oh my God. Oh my God.* He looked straight ahead when he heard a girl's voice coming towards him. The girl ran until she saw Jaiden and then came to a stop. She looked at him with her eyebrows furrowed in confusion.

"Everyone's gone," Laura said to the boy, who looked just as worried. It's all she could think, all she could say. *Everyone's gone. Everyone's gone.* The family that was sitting behind her. The guy in the booth controlling the ride. *Everyone's gone. Where did they go?*

"Yeah, Sophia, my friend, I don't know where she—" a new voice cut Jaiden off.

"Shut up, Eli!" Adam yelled as he stomped off the carousel. He stopped his angry march and looked over at Jaiden and Laura. "Who are you?" he asked rudely.

"Jaiden." *I don't like this kid,* Jaiden thought to himself after he answered.

"Laura," she said softly. *So weird.*

Elijah was a couple of steps behind Adam. "I'm Elijah," he said. "Or Eli or whatever and that's Adam."

Adam rolled his eyes and huffed, "What happened?" Adam asked Laura and Jaiden as if they weren't just as confused as he was.

"Hey!" The four of them turned to a girl running towards them from the other side of the ride. "Do any of you know what's going on?" Stella joined the group. She was slightly out of breath from desperate searching and increasing anxiety.

"Nope."

"No clue."

"Who are you?" Adam asked, still with an angry tone of voice.

"Stella." She inhaled sharply. "I was on this thing with my little cousins and now they're gone. I'm trying not to freak out, but I'm gonna get in so much trouble it's not even funny." She shook her hands to try to get rid of the jitters. "Yeah, same. I'm supposed to be home right now," Laura stressed. She felt around for her phone in her pockets. "Where's my phone?" She began looking around where she was standing as everyone else now realized they didn't have their phones either. Adam pretended to look around. Even in a crisis, he had to play a part.

"What is going on?" Elijah mumbled.

At the sound of a loud agonizing creak, all five heads turned towards the exit door of the carousel. A man, who hadn't been there the moment before, pushed it open. He had brown hair reaching the tops of his shoulders and wore a black top hat. His hands were resting in the pockets of his black pants, and the group did a double-take at his arms. The white of his T-Shirt made the colors in the ink of his tattoos stand out that much more. But that's not why the kids were shocked. This man's tattoos were moving, actually moving.

His left arm was completely dark blue down to his wrist. Planets and moons were spinning; twinkling stars were scattered among beautifully colored galaxies, pink, gray, and purple.

On the man's right arm from the elbow down to his wrist was the sea. Inside of the light blue waters were all different kinds of fish and sea creatures swimming around. From his elbow up, it looked like a rainforest. Beautiful green trees stood tall with birds flying around and jungle creatures perched on the branches.

How are they moving like that? Laura thought, too scared to say anything out loud.

Everyone was holding their breath, waiting to see what the man was going to do or say. All of them were silently hoping that someone else in the group would have the courage to take charge of the situation.

The man in the top hat smiled with dimples and said, "Hello! I'm glad you all arrived safely. How was the journey? Not too dizzying, I hope."

"What? What are you talking about?" Adam asked.

"Where are we? Who are you?" spoke Stella at the same time.

The man smiled and took a small step forward, sensing the wariness of the kids. "My name is R.L. Welcome to Cirque."

PART TWO

9. THE DINNER

R.L chuckled as voices rose at him all at once.

"What does R.L. stand for?" Elijah asked.

"What is Cirque?" Stella crossed her arms in frustration.

"Where are we? Like, where in the city are we?" Jaiden questioned.

"We're gonna die," Adam declared dramatically.

Laura just looked around, not sure what to do or say.

R.L. waited for them to be silent and then, "R.L. stands for ringleader, mostly. Really Loud, sometimes. Royal and Loyal, I suppose. Most things, except Ridiculous Loser—that's definitely not me," he winked at the group and chuckled at his own attempt at humor. "As for what Cirque is, you are standing in it." They looked around at the forest surrounding them and the freak show of a carousel. "This is Cirque Des Élus, Circus of the Chosen."

"A circus?" Elijah's voice squeaked a little so he coughed to try and cover it up. Adam snickered. "Shut up," Elijah grumbled.

"Yes, a circus," R.L. affirmed, drawing attention back to himself. "A circus in the city of Ekklesia."

They each tried to remember if they had ever heard of a city with that name.

"How did we get here?" Laura finally spoke up.

"I brought you here. My carousel helped, of course," R.L. gestured to the ride behind them.

"Where did everyone that was on the ride go?" Jaiden asked. *Poor Sophia, worst first date ever,* he thought.

"Yeah! What did you do to my cousins?" Stella demanded as she took a few steps closer to R.L.

Laura widened her eyes at the action. *That girl is crazy.*

"Stella, I promise you, everyone is okay. I can't explain everything to you, but I can tell you that everyone is fine," R.L. assured.

"How do you know my name?" Stella asked, now even more freaked out.

"I know all of your names. We've been expecting you here," R.L. smiled. "There's no need to be afraid."

The kids were silent, taking the absurdity of the moment in. The common thought among them was, *I must be dreaming.*

"This is weird," Adam shook his head, mumbling mostly to himself. He didn't trust the ringleader. He almost wanted to, for some strange reason, but he knew he couldn't. He had to be smart. He had to protect himself.

"I don't get it," Jaiden sighed. Where they stood didn't look like the same park he had been in earlier. He scanned the trees. They were different, wilder. The lamp posts looked taller and way older, with ivy winding around them. And there was something about the stars. At home, the stars were there if you looked up and wanted to see them. But here, it was like they were constantly in your peripheral vision. You saw their shine even if you weren't looking for it.

"This is some kind of dream," Stella muttered.

"Things will be explained in the best way they can be as time goes on," R.L.'s voice was soft and calm.

He waited as they all processed what was happening. He knew they were confused and having doubts. He smiled to himself and thought, *they always do.*

Elijah watched the other kids. He couldn't help but be excited, even though they were all skeptical. This was like the chance of a lifetime encounters he read about in books. He got pulled out of his sucky life and somehow ended up in a circus with a ringleader with moving tattoos—*awesome!*

"I'm sure this is a lot to take in. But, would you like to see the rest of Cirque? Maybe get something to eat?" R.L. proposed.

The group looked at each other as if trying to communicate without words about what they should do. *Do we go with the creepy guy? Do we run and try to find a way out?* R.L waited patiently for a response.

"Why not?" Elijah turned to the group and spoke timidly. They all huddled a little closer together on instinct. It felt like it was them against the crazy circus guy.

"'Cause he might be a creep and murderer and sell our body parts online or something," Stella whispered, trying to keep her voice low enough so the ringleader wouldn't hear.

"You watch too many crime shows," Adam laughed at her. She rolled her eyes.

"What else are we gonna do?" Elijah asked them.

"He's right," Jaiden agreed, surprising Elijah. "Maybe we can find a way home if we see more of whatever this place is."

"Whatever," was all Adam had to say.

Stella shrugged her shoulders.

Laura nodded her head when they all looked to her for an answer.

Adam followed behind the group with a little distance between them. Stella and Laura walked side by side, Elijah in front of them and Jaiden behind R.L., who led them. The gate to the carousel creaked again behind them as it closed, causing Laura to jump and gasp. Adam chuckled at her, earning an angry look from Stella. *What a jerk,* she thought.

R.L. elaborated as they walked, "Right now you are in the Side Show of Cirque, where all of our best freaks live," he said it lovingly, not like he was making fun of them, which Jaiden found interesting. "This is where you'll be staying while you're here. It's the most entertaining place you'll ever step foot in."

They neared a line of huge weeping willow trees that went on as far as the eye could see to the left and the right. Lights twinkled from within the leaves. The group stopped their steps when they neared a short brown door. Small flowers of varying colors covered the wood to the point where it could easily be hidden if you weren't looking for it. Boisterous laughter and music were being slightly muffled by the door.

R.L. Moved a bundle of red flowers to the side to reveal an old-fashioned door handle. A deep clicking sound signaled its opening. Each kid copied R.L.'s movement of ducking low as they walked through the doorway to avoid hitting their heads. The sound of instruments jamming, people laughing and shouting, and the smell of the fire from the fire pit hit them all at once.

"No way," Elijah gasped. His jaw dropped at the sight of

children playing together up ahead of them. One child had three legs, one child was floating a few inches off the ground, and another only wore shorts, showcasing clearly that every inch of him was sprouting brown hair.

"What are they?" Stella asked.

"Side Show performers," R.L. told her.

"But why do they look like that? How is that possible?" She couldn't take her eyes off them.

"It's how they were made," the ringleader smiled fondly. "This way." He led the group past the kids playing and towards the fire pit.

They passed a man who was swallowing swords for a group who cheered him on, a mermaid in a tank talking to a man and a woman who had tattoos and piercings everywhere except their eyeballs, and the roundest man they had ever seen laughing with a very, very, *very*, tiny woman as she stood in the palm of one of his hands.

Laura kept blinking, trying to make sure she saw right. Adam kept his eyes glued to the tiny woman, and Stella kept her eyes on the mermaid. Elijah didn't know where to look. He wanted to get a good view of it all.

"They're real?" Jaiden asked R.L.

"As real as you," he answered.

They came to a large fire pit where an even larger man sat. People were on benches all around him as he spoke.

"Clyde," R.L. called. The large man smiled and waved slowly, his hand bigger than any of the kids' heads.

"R.L., good to see you. Are these our new recruits?" Clyde leaned forward, inspecting the group before him.

"They are. We're going to get some dinner and get them settled in," R.L. said.

"Good, good. How freaked out are all of ya, then?" Clyde

spoke with an accent, but none of the kids could figure out what it was. All they could do was nod to his question, which made him laugh loudly, causing the ground to tremble. "I'll be seeing you around." Clyde winked.

R.L. continued walking. He turned and started up a dark gray stone path. Laura leaned over closer to the ground to make sure she was seeing correctly. Something twinkled on the path, something like stars, all along the winding way. R.L. held open a normal sized door for the group to walk through. They were now in a dark purple hallway accented with painted glittery gold swirls.

At the end of the hall, they turned left and entered a living room filled a few hundred people. Some played pool, others read by red brick fireplaces, and a few people admired the art and tapestries that hung on every inch of the walls. The people in this room didn't have interesting features like the Side Show performers. They looked normal, *but they couldn't be if they were in this circus,* Adam assumed.

Hanging from high ceilings was a collection of different lights, from huge gold chandeliers to single bulbs hanging by a wire. Lamps filled the room sitting on different tables; logs and glass and metal. Four brick fireplaces blazed, filling the room with a warm glow. Statues and sculptures stood beautifully.

"This room is the Commons. You're welcome here any time," R.L. explained. As they walked through the room, the people in it turned to smile and wave.

Elijah waved back while the others just looked at everyone skeptically.

"I swear, I've seen a scary movie like this once," Stella whispered to Laura. Laura creased her eyebrows in worry.

They walked out of the Commons and down a hallway

with stained glass murals on the walls and a ceiling that depicted a circus show. All different acts were represented, even Side Show performers. Elijah peeked down the different hallways connected to the one they were in, but he couldn't see anything.

"Here is where we dine as a family. We have a late dinner prepared for you," R.L. said as they continued straight and entered a large room.

Tall windows from floor to ceiling surrounded one giant table. The table had hundreds of chairs around it of different styles. It was the length of the room with other rectangle tables coming out of it at different places. Gold chandeliers hung from a mosaic ceiling of red and white stripes.

The group sat down. Their grumbling stomachs echoed throughout the dining room. A variety of food sat in front of them; spaghetti, sushi, tacos, pizza-they looked at the ringleader unsure of what to do next.

"Dig in," he encouraged. Jaiden was the first to start putting food on his plate, and then the rest followed. R.L. leaned against the table and watched in amusement. He said, "Eat all you want, and then we have one more stop before you can settle in for the night."

"What stop?" Elijah asked aloud what everyone was wondering.

"To be Marked," the ringleader flashed them a wide smile.

10. THE CHAOS

"All we have to do is cause chaos," the Shadow King spoke to the crowd of figures before him. They cheered at their leader's words.

"Yeah, chaos!" The crowd began to shout over each other, like hyper children all excited about the same thing.

The King spoke again, his voice booming over the other shadows, "Chaos in their *circus*," he spat. "It will crumble in on itself. Cirque Des Èlus will be ours."

The shadows screeched in glee. The broken bleachers they stood in shook with the force of their stomps and shouts. Their leader addressed them from the middle of their black and white circus ring. The ripped-up tent trembled above them. The Shadow King's face distorted into something too wicked to be considered a smile, white eyes gleamed with mischief.

Cirque would surely fall.

All they needed was a little chaos.

11. THE MARKING

No matter how many times R.L. was asked what he meant by his "to be Marked" comment, he wouldn't give a straight answer. Each kid felt their nerves in different ways–sweaty palms, twisted stomachs, rampant overthinking–as they walked down a dimly lit hallway somewhere in Cirque.

"This is it, this is when we die," said Adam as he walked with his hands in his hoodie pocket. R.L. just laughed lightly at the comment and Stella and Jaiden told Adam to shut up.

They stopped in front of a door. A short man with a round belly and curly brown hair opened it for them with a smile. "I'm Barnaby," he introduced himself.

"Barnaby is my best friend and best assistant," R.L. patted Barnaby on the back. "Anything you need, he can help."

"It's so good to meet you. Come on in," Barnaby stood to the side of the door so they could enter.

They followed R.L. into the room and Barnaby closed the door behind them. It was dark except for a few candles that hung on the gray stone walls. A white stone podium stood in the center of the room, and there was a hatch in the ceiling above it.

"You can stand here," Barnaby instructed everyone where to go. Laura and Stella stood to the right of the podium, Elijah and Jaiden to the left, and Adam stood behind it facing Barnaby who was now near the door.

"This is creepy," Stella told the ringleader. She tried to come off as brave even though she was terrified inside. *What are they going to do to us?* Her mind panicked.

"I'm sorry for that," R.L. told her, and then he looked at Barnaby. "Maybe we could find a less *creepy* way to do this." He emphasized creepy as if no one had ever described the process like that before.

Barnaby nodded and tapped his forehead, "Mental note taken."

"Now," R.L. looked at the wide eyes before him. "This will not hurt you. You will feel a slight tingle but it is harmless."

"What's gonna happen?" Jaiden asked.

"A tingle?" Adam looked at the others to see if they were as weirded out as he was.

Instead of answering their concerns, R.L. pulled down a lever to his right that opened the hatch above the podium. A breeze blew quickly into the room and a single beam of moonlight hit the podium and then reflected off into five more beams. Everyone held their breath as the light hit each of the kids in the base of their neck and disappeared into their skin.

"What the–" Stella let her words fall as she watched the bright light shoot down both her arms.

Laura shook her left arm when goosebumps rose all over it. She gasped when the moonlight revealed a tattoo on the skin of her inner forearm. She looked to R.L., then back at her arm, and then back at R.L.

He explained, "Each mark represents the circus act you were born for."

Stella looked at her arm and saw a horse with its legs bent like it was running. "What the heck am I supposed to do?" she asked, her loud voice echoing off the walls of the small room.

"Equestrian act," Barnaby told her softly as he looked over her shoulder.

"Acrobat," R.L. said to Adam. Adam had pushed his sleeve up and was staring intently at the ink on his arm that looked like a person doing a backflip.

"An acrobat here too," Barnaby called when he saw Elijah's mark.

"Great," Adam huffed.

Elijah felt dread in his stomach for the first time during this whole circus ordeal. *Why did I have to get stuck with Adam?*

"Clown? For real?" Laura scowled. An outline of a clown face stared back at her.

"Congratulations," R.L. told her, smiling.

She didn't find it amusing. *A freaking clown?* Was all she could think as she continued to stare at her arm.

"What am I?" Jaiden questioned, looking at his arm in confusion.

"Human Cannonball," R.L. answered when he looked at the marking.

"What?" he exclaimed.

R.L. and Barnaby chuckled.

"So, what now?" Elijah asked.

"You will be trained in each of these acts, and you will become masters of them," R.L. said.

"I must've taken drugs or something by accident. This is crazy," mumbled Stella.

"You expect me to be shot out of a cannon?" Jaiden gawked.

"I assure you all," R.L. spoke seriously although he was doing his best not to laugh at their reactions. "You were born for this. Born to do each of those acts marked on your arms. It is destiny. It is your birthright. And we will begin tomorrow." The kids just looked to the ringleader with dumbfounded expressions. He clasped his hands together in finality. "Now, I will show you where you'll be staying."

"CAN YOU BELIEVE ALL OF THIS?" Stella asked Laura. They each sat on their own bed and stared at the ceiling of the train car they were in.

R.L. had led them back to the Side Show and they walked down a path to the left of the fire pit. There was a long train that went on for miles. It had enormous train cars painted beautifully, some with animals depicted on the side, others with faces, and some with just words. The train tracks it sat on were completely overtaken by grass like the train hadn't moved in years and years.

R.L. encouraged the group to try and get some sleep. He bid them goodnight and then disappeared, leaving behind a cloud of glittery red smoke. The kids didn't even bat an eye. It's not like it was the craziest thing that had happened so far.

The boys were all staying in the car next to Stella and Laura's. Their beds were spread out with a bathroom in the corner and a trunk with each kids' initials on it filled with clothes at the foot of the beds.

"I don't know," Laura answered Stella. "I don't know." She couldn't think of anything else to say.

"Yeah, hopefully, we'll just wake up in the morning in our beds at home, and we'll remember this as a crazy dream," Stella said.

"Maybe this circus thing, maybe it won't be so bad," Laura whispered. She didn't really mean to say it. It slipped out making her realize just how tired she was.

"If it's even real," was the last thing Stella said before they both fell asleep.

As the Side Show and the rest of Cirque dozed off peacefully, a cold wind blew through the circus. Down the hallways, through the Commons, in and out of the dining room. R.L. sat straight up in his office chair, and Barnaby stopped speaking mid-sentence. Both men stayed completely still, feeling the breeze that deviously snuck through their home.

CLANK!

Jaiden fell off of his bed when something hit the side of the train car. He stood up and looked over to see Adam and Elijah. They were both awake and equally freaked out.

CLANK!

Laura screamed as the sound came again. It was like something huge was smashing right into the outside metal wall. Stella ran over and sat on Laura's bed. They held each other's hands tightly.

CLANK!

By now, the whole Side Show was awake and terrified. The horrible loud noise kept happening. The train cars shook with the impact. **CLANK! CLANK! CLANK!** The noise was coming from every angle, and laughter started happening with it. Echoing, taunting chaotic laughter.

All at once, every single door on the train slid open violently causing everyone to scream. Adam clenched his fists and stood up, trying to see outside without moving closer to the door. Jaiden still stood beside his bed. Elijah held his covers tight in his hands.

There was a thick black smoke hovering right outside.

"What is that?" Jaiden asked quietly like he was scared it would hear.

"It feels bad," Elijah whispered. He didn't know how he knew, but something felt horribly wrong about whatever that smoke was. Everything up until this point seemed peaceful and okay, but now, this seemed threatening.

Slowly the smoke began to enter into every train car. Most of it moved against the walls, while a small cloud moved forward in the center.

Laura and Stella both scooted as far back as they could. Their bodies hitting the headboard of the bed they wished would swallow them up and take them far away from whatever was coming towards them. Their stomachs twisted up with anxiety. The smoke got closer and closer, and muffled voices flowed out of it.

Laura could've sworn she could hear her parents' voices, loud and arguing. The more she focused on trying to figure out what she was hearing, the clearer it became. It *was* her mom and dad fighting. She remembered it, clear as day. It was the last fight they had in their house. It was the night her dad walked out, and things changed forever.

It was the night her mom locked herself in her bathroom and cried all night. She had turned on the shower to try to drown out the noise, but Laura still heard the sobs through the walls. It's all she could hear. Laura was sitting on the floor of her room just listening to her mother cry and thinking about what she could've done differently to help her parents stay together.

"You idiot! You never listen to anything I say!" Adam gasped at his mother's voice. Her screaming was coming right from the black thing that kept inching closer and closer. He looked over to see if Jaiden and Elijah had heard her too, but they both stared into the smoke like they were lost in it.

"Why can't you just do what I tell you? Why do you have to make things so hard?" Adam could see his mom now as she yelled. He sat on their couch. He was back in their living room. She just kept yelling, the same things she always said. He just sat there and took all the anger she was throwing at him, wanting nothing more than to be anyone else.

Jaiden felt ashamed as his father yelled. He could see it all in the smoke. He sat at their kitchen table, and his parents stood in front of him. They were both so angry, but he had no idea why. "Why would you risk everything? Do you know what we went through to get here?" Jaiden wanted to hide. "Everything we have done has been for your future!" He was so embarrassed. *I'm a failure. I'm a disappointment. I'm letting them down.* He thought to himself over and over again. *I'm a failure. I'm a disappointment. I'm letting them down.*

"Mom? Mom!" Stella yelled. She had seen her mom in the black smoke. She had been standing right in front of her. Stella smiled and called out for her, but her mom didn't seem to realize she was there. She turned and started walking away. Stella yelled after her but she never looked back. "Mom! Mom!" She tried to run and catch up to the retreating figure, but it was no use. No matter how far Stella ran, she could never catch up.

Beep. Beep. Beep. It's all Elijah could hear. He stared into the black, into nothingness. It was like he was blind, but the beeping of a machine assaulted his ears. He recognized the sound. Beep. Beep. Beep. It was the machine at the hospital, the one that tracked the rhythm of his dad's heart. He would never forget that sound. It haunted him. The short beeps reminded him that his dad was still alive, for now.

And then, in the darkness of the smoke, Elijah heard the worst sound. The one, drawn-out beep that declared to the world that his dad was never waking up. But this time, the sound never stopped. Elijah couldn't make it stop. There was no machine to turn off, no hospital to leave. He was trapped in this nothingness with his ears aching.

Beeeeeeeeeeep.

12. THE HALL OF CHOICE

R.L. appeared in front of the train. His anger rose as he saw how the Shadows were almost completely overtaking it, each train car barely visible through the smoke. He could hear the cries and pleads of his Side Show freaks and his new recruits.

"No!" R.L.'s voice boomed. Red light, like lightning, hit the shadows and ripped through their smoky bodies, breaking them apart. They rapidly began uncovering the train and forming together into one shape that materialized in front of the ringleader.

As the train cars were freed of the Shadows, those within them that had succumbed were snapped out of the fear they had been trapped in. Everyone peered out of the doors to see R.L. standing face to face with a shadowy figure.

R.L. looked to see his new recruits staring at him, most with tears still in their eyes. The ringleader clenched his fists in fury at the sight. He spoke to the Shadow before him, "How dare you?"

The Shadow snorted and laughed. "You make it too easy, *ringleader*," the Shadow spat and inched closer.

"Get. Out. Now." R.L.'s voice left no room for argument, and the Shadow began fading like it couldn't help but do what it was told.

"I'll be back," its once strong voice was now coming through in static, like a radio station losing the signal. The Shadow flickered for a moment and then it was gone.

R.L. stared for a second longer, his face depicting so much anger it made everyone glad they weren't going to be on the receiving end of it. He then took a deep breath and looked around him to his people, all waiting for comfort and answers.

"I am so sorry for the events that have taken place. This is the second time that the Shadows have intruded, but we will do everything we can to make it be the last. Please, rest, and when the time is right we will discuss a plan of action." The Side Show nodded and went back into their homes, closing the train car doors.

R.L. walked up in between the cars where his new recruits stood warily. They all looked between each other and to the ringleader. Adam had rubbed the tears from his eyes viciously. Laura's cheeks were still wet, but she didn't care. Stella crossed her arms over her chest, the feeling of abandonment and loneliness consuming her like it always did when it came to her mother. Jaiden and Elijah had empty expressions like they had shut down for the moment, unable to cope otherwise.

"Again, I am so sorry this happened," the ringleader began.

"What were those things?" Adam interrupted.

"Shadow People. They are evil, and they know how to get in our heads and cause pain."

"Why?" Laura's voice was small, almost nonexistent. Her hands trembled slightly.

"The more afraid, angry, and hurt we are, the stronger they become. They want to destroy Cirque. They have been relentless lately." R.L. took a step forward. "You really are safe here. I will protect you. I didn't warn you properly about them, and you weren't ready to resist them. I apologize. But it will not happen again."

"We could've resisted them?" Jaiden asked, his eyes now more focused on the present moment.

"We will talk more about it tomorrow. For now, please get back to sleep. You need to rest. You begin training tomorrow." R.L. gave a small smile.

The group nodded and turned to go to their beds without saying a word. R.L. felt a pang to his heart, knowing that they were going to sleep with what the Shadows showed them on replay in their mind. The doors to their train cars closed.

"Sleep well," R.L. whispered. None of the kids saw the red glitter mist that hovered over each of them that night. They slept peacefully and protected, not a single nightmare.

"CAN YOU PASS THE SYRUP?" Stella asked Jaiden.

The group sat at breakfast in the dining hall the next morning. The voices of the Side Show up and about had woken everyone up. Barnaby had knocked on their doors shortly after, offering to take them to breakfast.

"Last night was creepy, huh?" Elijah said. None of them

had spoken about it yet. Mostly because they wanted to pretend it didn't happen.

"Understatement," Laura said.

"Did you guys," Jaiden paused, regretting what he was about to say. "Never mind." If he didn't want to talk about what he saw, he was sure they didn't either.

"What? See stuff?" Stella said with more attitude than she meant. Her mother's face was the first thing on her mind that morning. She had slept well, had good dreams, actually, but as soon as she woke up, she saw her mom's face and then her mom's back as she walked away.

"Yeah," Jaiden answered tentatively.

"I did," Laura stared at her breakfast as she spoke. "I saw my parents. They were fighting. It was a memory, though. But it was like I was reliving it."

"It was sort of like that for me," Stella explained. "It wasn't exactly a memory, but it felt real, way too real."

"Same for me," said Jaiden. He wasn't about to go into details, though.

"Adam, Eli? How about you?" Laura questioned.

Adam waited to see if Eli was going to say anything. When he didn't seem like he was going to, Adam just shrugged his shoulders and looked at his plate. He wasn't gonna tell these strangers the things his mom said about him. They'd laugh. Or worse, agree. He continued to eat.

"I," Elijah started talking. "I didn't see anything. It was all black and empty for me, but I heard stuff." He pushed the food on his plate around with his fork. He didn't have an appetite.

"I saw my parents," Jaiden said quickly before he could change his mind about talking, "they were mad at me for something, and they were basically telling me how much of a disappointment I am."

Everyone looked at him, shocked. They couldn't believe he was telling them something so personal. They had only known each other for like a day.

"I saw my mom," Stella offered. Maybe talking about it would help. "She was just walking away from me. I don't think she could see me. Pretty accurate," she scoffed.

Adam continued stuffing his face. *No way am I doing this,* he thought.

"I heard my dad dying," Elijah whispered. He didn't have to look up to know everyone was staring.

Even Adam looked at him like he didn't hate him for a second. Elijah wasn't going to elaborate. So, after a minute everyone continued eating in silence all curious to know each other's stories.

"Good morning," R.L. greeted the group and sat down with them. The dining room was starting to empty out. "I hope you all slept well last night." They nodded in response. "Great, today you begin training." This statement caused the kids to come to life. The energy they had had the day before coming back as they fired questions at the ringleader.

"You were serious?"

"Training, how?"

"Who's training us?"

"You weren't kidding?"

Laura was the only one who sat in silence as she looked at the clown marking on her arm. *Ridiculous,* she shook her head.

R.L. laughed, his whole body moving with the sound. Without realizing it, the group relaxed. The ringleader just had something about him. Something that made everyone feel like it was going to be okay. He stood up and began to leave the dining room. He turned to his recruits. "Come with me."

They followed him down the hallways into the Commons. They walked up a staircase that had gone unnoticed before. At the top of it was a vibrant red wooden door with a large gold *C painted in the middle.* R.L. opened it up and the group entered another hallway.

"This is the Hall of Choice." R.L. stood in the middle of the hall and gestured to three doors on his right and three on his left. On one wall was a door that looked like it was made completely of gold. R.L. gestured to it and said, "the Door Of Desire."

"That" –R.L. pointed to the door next to the Door of Desire– "is the Door of Need." This door was made of split, weak wood. It was barely holding onto the hinges. It seemed like it had been there forever. Through the many cracks of the door, a light was leaking.

"Door of Opportunity," R.L. remarked. The next door was completely chrome. It could've passed as a mirror.

"The Lost Room," the ringleader named the door on the other side of the Hall of Choice. "Where our dreams and such go."

"And that door?" Adam asked. He stared at a towering black metal door. It had heavy chains crisscrossing it and multiple locks above the door handle. A barely visible red hue was coming off it and voices could be heard from behind it.

"That is where the Shadows come from," R.L. said each word carefully, letting it sink in. The group looked at him bewildered. "Some call it the Dark Door, some call it the

Door of Shadows. I keep them close to keep them in check," he told them.

"Well, great job," Adam muttered, looking at the door again. The sight of it made his skin crawl.

R.L. just smiled and started towards the Door of Shadows. "We continue this way."

No one said a word, but they all kept as far away from the Shadow door as possible.

They walked down two more hallways. One with different picture frames lining the walls filled with photos of groups of people. Some were simple modern square frames and others were oval with intricate gold designs. In every photo, the people were smiling and standing in front of red and white stripes.

The other hall had dozens of different tapestries hanging on the walls, all of them depicting people living life in a beautiful city. The floor of the hallway was a clean white and gray marble with gold specks scattered throughout. The footsteps of the group echoed. R.L. stayed silent, letting them process what they were seeing. *This place is beautiful,* Laura thought. She couldn't deny the splendor of Cirque.

At the end of the hall, they walked through thick blue velvet curtains and entered a circus ring. The kids looked around, taking their surroundings in. Bleachers lined the ring, giant posters showcasing different acts hung above them. Lion tamer, tightrope walker, fire breather, and more.

The room was filled with people all smiling and waving to the group. They were all doing different things, stretching, doing gymnastics. There were even people towering above them practicing the trapeze. Elijah gulped, thankful he wasn't marked with that circus act.

R.L. led them towards the bleachers to their left. They

stopped in front of four people who all smiled. "These are your trainers," R.L. told them. "Laura, this is Etta."

Etta was an older lady with dark skin and a beautiful afro that bounced slightly when she moved. She stepped forward and hugged Laura. Laura stood unmoving, caught off guard by this woman and her forwardness. "It's an honor," Etta said.

Laura smiled, *she seems nice.*

R.L. gestured to the man that had been standing to the left of Etta. "This is Hank. He will be training Elijah and Adam in acrobatics." Hank reached out and shook Eli and Adam's hands. He looked old enough to be their dads. *His arms are huge,* Elijah observed. Adam crossed his arms over his chest, *this is so stupid.*

"Jaiden," R.L. said and pointed to the next person in line. He was a young guy with a shaved head. "This is Arlo, your fellow human cannonball."

"What's up, man?" Arlo did some sort of handshake with Jaiden, who went along with it, trying not to embarrass himself.

"And this is Julie," R.L. introduced the last woman. She shook Stella's hand, knowing a hug would put off the already cautious girl.

"It's a pleasure to meet you," Julie's voice was raspy and warm. Stella nodded her head but didn't say anything.

"Well," the ringleader said to the recruits and their trainers, "time to get started."

13. THE JUMP

"**T**he key to acrobatics," Hank said, "is trust."

Elijah and Adam kept their distance and barely looked at each other. If they did make eye contact, Adam would roll his eyes, and Elijah would avert his as quickly as possible. It was impossible for Hank not to notice.

"Trust," Elijah echoed, taking a mental note.

Adam snickered and shook his head.

The boys had followed to the other side of the circus ring where a group of people were doing flips, handstands, and other tricks off the bleachers, single-person trampolines, and even each other. One guy was doing a perfect handstand, holding himself up with one hand that rested on the top of another guy's head.

"We work off of each other, so we gotta work together." Hank stopped to face his recruits. He crossed his muscular arms over his chest and raised an eyebrow. "Should be easy for you two, yeah?" Something told the boys their instructor already knew the answer to that.

"What are we going to be doing? I've never done a flip in my life, or a handstand, or anything like that," Elijah said. He was starting to sweat.

Adam looked at Hank for an answer. He was feeling the same nerves as Elijah but was trying his best not to show it.

"You were marked for this. You'll be surprised how natural it comes. You were born for this." Hank continued walking toward the trampolines.

"I don't know about that," Adam chuckled.

"First, we jump." Hank pointed out the trampolines.

"This is so stupid," grumbled Adam, *and embarrassing,* he thought.

Hank just smiled, "Jump."

STELLA WALKED beside Julie as they left the circus ring and ended up in a hallway with several different colored doors. Julie spoke as they walked, "each of these doors leads to a different animal's land."

"What do you mean?" Stella asked. Julie wriggled her eyebrows like she was about to reveal a big secret and opened an orange door. They peeked through it, and Stella gasped.

An endless blue sky and a scorching sun hung above wild grass, trees, and a bundle of rocks where a pride of lions lounged in the distance. Julie closed her eyes and relished in the sun. Stella kept blinking. She couldn't tell if she was really seeing what she thought she was seeing.

"I don't get it."

Julie just laughed, and they stepped back into the hallway. She closed the orange door, and they continued walking. She pointed to a door to her right, "Through there you'll meet our elephant family in an Indian sun," she stuck her thumb towards a door on her left, "and through that one there is the biggest backyard you've ever seen with everything a dog could want. Our animal performers are very happy here at Cirque. They all have their own space, their own habitat."

"How is this even possible?" Stella cringed at her own pitchy voice. *Relax,* she told herself, *just chill.*

Julie just laughed some more. "Sweetie, soon you'll get tired of asking that question cause no one's gonna give you an answer you'll be satisfied with. Come on." She turned the knob on a distressed black door and pushed it open.

Whoa, Stella tried to say it out loud but nothing came out of her mouth. Blue mountains reached high into the sky with wisps of clouds gathered at their peaks. Yellow grass came up to her knees, and she could hear the sound of horses neighing and galloping even though she couldn't see them. Their movement and calls echoed through the valley.

Julie led Stella to stand on a hill overlooking a winding river. Stella jumped at the sudden sound of a wolf whistle coming from Julie.

"Ow," Stella grumbled while rubbing her ears, earning another laugh from Julie.

A beautiful black and white horse galloped at full speed towards them. Stella flinched back and hid behind her trainer, but Julie stood still. The horse slowed to a stop a few feet in front of them and bowed his head a little.

"Hey, baby," Julie whispered. She rubbed its forehead and the side of its face. "Stella meet Domino. Domino, this is Stella." Julie moved out of the way, so Stella was standing right in front of Domino. "He's a good boy," Julie insisted.

"Hi," the word came out as more of a breath, but Stella couldn't help it. She had never been this close to a horse before. The most she knew about horses came from a cartoon movie she had watched as a kid.

"Reach out slowly and rub his head, nothing to be afraid of."

After a minute of contemplation, Stella did as Julie said. Domino bowed his head, and Stella petted him, and she felt herself smile. Her shoulders relaxed a bit, and her breathing evened out.

"Nothing to be afraid of," Julie said again. "We're gonna start you off working with this guy since he's more experienced. And then, you'll choose your own."

Stella followed Julie's gaze to a group of horses in the distance eating grass. They were all different colors and patterns. A few baby horses ran around like they were playing tag with each other.

"So I have to like ride horses?" Stella asked. She kept rubbing Domino's face. *I guess he's not that bad.* She smiled at the whinnying sound that came from him. Stella whipped her head to face Julie when she answered her question.

"Ride, stand on their backs while they run, do some tricks," Julie said casually, smirking at the way Stella's eyes widened. "Easy, peasy."

"I'M SUPPOSED to climb into this thing and then get shot out of it?" Jaiden asked Arlo.

A black cannon sat in front of them, pointed towards the top of the tent. Two red wheels, as tall as Jaiden, were attached to the cannon's sides. Red stars were painted all over the black cylinder.

"Pretty much," Arlo stated nonchalantly. He beamed at

the cannon, a light in his eyes like he was reminiscing. "It's exhilarating, a rush like no other."

"Where do you land?" Jaiden looked around, but there was no type of trampoline or anything near them.

"When the time comes, there will be a net, and hopefully, you'll land in it."

"Hopefully?" Jaiden yelled more than asked.

Arlo winked. "Climb up there and look inside."

"No thanks," Jaiden said with a smile.

"Ha ha." Arlo walked to the other side of the cannon with Jaiden following. There was a ladder leaning up against it. "Climb up and look inside. I promise you won't be catapulted into the air just yet. We gotta get you familiar with the cannon and mechanics first. And we have to spend some time weightlifting."

"Why weightlifting?" Jaiden asked as he slowly climbed the ladder. He looked around to make sure there was no one around to accidentally fire up the cannon.

"We need to have strong back, knee, and core strength. When we're inside, we clench our bodies to stay as rigid as possible during the blast," Arlo explained.

"Oh," Jaiden's mind filled with things he wanted to say, but he kept his mouth shut. They were probably just messing with him after all. There's no way they were really gonna make him do this.

"What do you see?" Arlo asked once Jaiden was at the top of the ladder.

Jaiden leaned forward and looked down the muzzle. The lights shining in the circus ring illuminated the inside. The cannon was empty, of course, and narrow. It looked like there were metal springs at the bottom of it.

"Um, springs? At the bottom?" Jaiden looked back at Arlo.

"That's right, here's a secret, there's not actually gunpowder and a match. You're not technically *fired* out of the cannon."

"Well, that's good news." Jaiden's heart slowed it's racing a bit.

"Yeah, it's a spring that launches your body to top speed in about one-fifth of a second." His trainer smiled and stood with his hands on his hips, perfectly at ease. Jaiden's heart started up again.

Jaiden started climbing down as he spoke, "how long have you been doing this?"

Arlo made a motorboat sound with his lips. "Long, long, long time."

"You don't look that old," Jaiden told him. His feet hit the ground, and he couldn't have been happier. *Definitely like it down here better.*

"Thanks, come on we'll go to the weight room." Jaiden followed him out of the circus ring.

"Were you scared at first?" Jaiden asked as they walked.

"Of course! I'd be concerned if you weren't scared," Arlo laughed. "But you gotta get over the fear," Arlo faced Jaiden, "and the only way to get over the fear of the cannon is to climb into it."

"So, no offense," Laura started.

"Usually, that's a warning that you're about to be offended," Etta joked.

"Right," Laura decided not to continue with what she was saying. She didn't want to be rude, but this clown thing was ridiculous. Did they expect her to wear face paint and crazy-looking clothes? Ride around on a tiny bike or make balloon animals? *No freaking way, I won't do it, I won't.*

"I know you might have some preconceived notions on what it means to be a clown. Probably have some images in your head already. Those are stereotypes, love. Never good to believe something about people before you meet them yourself," Etta said gently.

"Sorry," Laura stuffed her hands in her pockets.

"No worries," Etta winked.

They had walked through a thick navy blue curtain. The way the light hit the silver stars on it made it seem like they were actually twinkling. *Maybe they are, wouldn't be surprised.* Laura looked around what seemed to be the backstage of the circus. Wooden beams, ropes, and unused lights were in every nook and cranny. People were moving, painting, and building props. Laura noticed a tattoo of a needle and thread on the forearm of a girl sewing some sort of costume.

Laura opened her mouth to ask Etta about it, but her instructor beat her to the punch. "Even the behind the scenes is considered a circus act. Nothing would be possible without those who build and create. It's an honorable marking. Hey, Lauren," Etta waved at the girl.

She waved back and smiled at both of them.

They walked for another minute before they entered the most colorful room Laura had ever seen. Different fabrics were draped all around and every piece of furniture seemed out of place and perfectly belonging all at once.

"Welcome to Clown Alley," Etta said.

Laura gaped.

Upbeat music matched the joyful mood everyone seemed to be in. Some people were sat in chairs in front of mirrors, putting on tons of makeup. Others were juggling, trying on costumes, and practicing jokes on each other. Laughter was everywhere. Laura felt her lips slightly turn up in a hint of a smile. It was impossible not to feel the positivity around her.

"Hey!" A teenage boy ran up and affectionately wrapped his long arms around Etta.

"Laura," Etta chuckled and put her arm around the boy's waist, "this is my son Amos." Amos was tall and skinny with an afro like his mom's.

"Nice to meet you," Laura said politely.

"You too, welcome to the clown life," he grinned goofily.

"Thanks," Laura smiled, trying to seem excited, but the way Etta and Amos laughed she knew they saw right through it.

"Let me show you around." Etta linked their arms together as she gave her the tour. Amos followed close behind.

"This is where we get geared up. Make-up, hair, costume —the works. We practice in the circus ring, but we'll get to that. First, I want you to get settled and understand what it is we do," Etta waved to people they passed as she spoke. "Let's sit." Etta led them to a dark purple velvet couch.

"We do a lot of different things as clowns," Amos spoke quickly like he was so excited to get all of the words out. "Some of us are on the floor, that's what we call the circus ring, and we perform for the big crowd." He spread his arms apart as he spoke. Laura smiled at his dramatic way of talking. "Some of us are carpet clowns. We walk around in the audience and perform. Make balloon animals, do magic tricks, things like that. Mama here is the boss clown."

"What will I have to do?" Laura asked. She just wanted to get this over with, whatever they wanted her to do.

"That's for you to decide," Etta told her. "You'll figure it out as you see the different aspects of the clown life. You'll find your spot."

"Cool." Laura bounced her knee and looked around the room.

"Laura," Etta got her attention, "you were marked for this. You will come to enjoy it and understand it."

"I don't get what's to understand, and I'm really not trying to be rude or anything. But like, I don't wanna be a clown. I don't wanna look ridiculous and make a fool out of myself," Laura rushed the words out of her mouth.

"Why?"

Laura scrunched her face in confusion, "What?"

"Why don't you want to look ridiculous and make a fool out of yourself if it's for a good cause?" Etta questioned softly.

"Good cause? What good cause?" Laura leaned back into the couch, expecting a long explanation.

"'Laughter is the best medicine,' I'm sure you've heard that said, yes?"

Laura nodded.

"Have you ever laughed so hard it hurt? Had such a good laugh it made you giggle weeks later?" Etta asked.

Laura nodded and smiled, remembering moments with her friends.

"Every time we perform, we have the opportunity to help sick people." Etta leaned forward. "People who might go their whole day, maybe a whole week, without proper laughter. Without laughing so hard, it makes their stomach hurt or brings tears to their eyes. That type of laughter, any type of laughter, is medicine to the soul. Proper clowns, bring laughter. We bring medicine to the sick people who sit in our bleachers."

14. THE STORY

"What did he say we were doing?" Laura whispered to Stella. They walked side by side behind the boys. They followed R.L. from the dining hall to the Side Show.

"A bonfire," Stella told her and shrugged her shoulders.

They had finished training, rested in the commons, and then ate dinner. A few of the circus performers had joined them. A Lion Tamer named Wyatt, a Tightrope Walker named Milo, and some people from the Side Show.

"I told you that we would speak more about the Shadows today. After last night you deserve an explanation," R.L. spoke.

They walked through the door to the Side Show. An acoustic guitar was being strummed lightly over hushed voices of the crowd. *I didn't know this place knew how to be quiet,* Jaiden thought. R.L. led them to the fire pit where Clyde sat. The Side Show and all the other Cirque performers gathered around on benches, chairs, and the grass. There were even a few sitting on the thick branches of the trees above. The ringleader and the kids settled onto a bench to Clyde's right.

"Clyde is going to tell us a story," R.L. whispered and winked.

Elijah leaned forward with his elbows on his knees, Adam yawned, and Jaiden looked around, still perplexed over the three-legged boy that sat on the other side of Clyde, *is it comfortable to sit like that?* He thought. Stella and Laura shared a *"this is going to be interesting"* look.

"Hello, family," Clyde greeted the crowd that surrounded him. More people came in and joined as he spoke. "Last night, we suffered an attack." There were some groans and disgruntled comments. "Our ringleader has asked me to remind us all of the Shadows' story because their story is just as much *our* story. We know that the Door of Shadows resides in our circus, and we have a sworn duty to protect Cirque and Ekklesia."

"Ekklesia?" Jaiden whispered to R.L. who sat right beside him.

"You'll see," was all the ringleader said.

Clyde continued, "Long ago, the Shadows were a part of this circus." Clyde moved his hand over the orange fire in front of him, and as he did, the color changed to a dark red.

Okay, that's cool, Adam thought. He straightened up and watched closely.

"They were marked just like you and me," Clyde showed off his inner forearm and the inked outline of a book. "But they began to want more. More responsibility, more cheers from the crowds, more spotlight." The fire was then white and Stella could've sworn she heard the faint cheering of a crowd coming from it. "The more that they craved these things, the more that they put others down to try and get them, the darker the light of their mark became." Within the white flames, a dark smoke began to swirl. It spread and spread until the fire was black.

"The moonlight that had sealed the mark on their arm was being covered, hidden. The longer they tried to do acts they were not marked for, the more their chosen mark faded from their skin. And before they knew it, their entire being was rid of the moonlight it once held. Now, they were just a shadow of who they were meant to be," Clyde's voice was heavy with grief.

Elijah looked at R.L. There were tears falling slowly down his cheeks. His hands that were gripped around the cane he carried trembled. The ringleader stared into the black fire and clenched his jaw. Elijah couldn't tell if he looked more sad or more angry, it was probably an even split.

Clyde moved his hand over the fire again and different shades of red broke up the black. "Our ringleader did all he could. Some were saved from a life in the shadows." Clyde looked around the crowd, nodding to the few who it had been. They had tears in their eyes as well. "But, some were not. And others chose to turn away from Cirque and join them in attempting to destroy our circus." Clyde shook his head, "R.L. and others fought to get them out of Cirque and away from the city they were bent on taking over. In the Hall of Choice a door was added that day." Within the fire, the Hall of Choice was revealed. Like a movie scene, the fire slowly zoomed into the Dark Door.

"Though they are Shadows, underneath it all, there is still a mark. A mark that was made with the moonlight that shines on Cirque, on Ekklesia, and the world." Clyde looked to the group of kids who were all entranced by his tale. "There is always hope. We've seen it. But, we must also be ready. Any one of us could become like them. All it takes is a choice." Laura shivered. "And any one of them could join us again right here. All it takes is a choice." Clyde looked to R.L.

The ringleader smiled and stood, still with wet cheeks. He looked over the crowd for a moment before speaking, "Cirque will not crumble."

Elijah was startled when Cirque broke out in shouts and claps. Together, their stomping feet formed into a consistent rhythm. R.L. continued, "Ekklesia will stay protected. Cirque will stand the test of time as it has already. And our door will remain open to new recruits." He smiled at the five kids staring at him in awe and confusion.

Everyone stood up and cheered and hugged each other. The band began playing, and a party broke out. Clyde's fire returned to its normal color. He laughed and joked with a group of children that ran up to him. R.L. turned to the group, who remained seated.

"So, the Shadows, they were a part of Cirque," Jaiden clarified.

"Yes," R.L. nodded.

"And, the mark on our arms," Jaiden let his sentence hang.

"Is made with and full of moonlight like theirs were." R.L.'s smile fell. "But they allowed other things to cover it up and morph themselves into Shadows. They were trying to be everything else besides what they were marked for. They didn't think it was enough."

"Dang," Laura couldn't believe someone would want to hurt this place. It might have been weird, but they all seemed like such good people.

"And what? The Shadows wanna destroy Cirque? Just cause they think they can?" Stella asked.

"Yes, they just want to take. Take the circus, take the city of Ekklesia, and take as many people with them. They would love nothing more than to take you. To have you join them." R.L. knelt in front of them and looked at each person in the eye. Even Adam didn't try to look away. He could feel the heaviness of this moment. "They try almost every time I have new recruits. The Shadows have a way of getting into your head. It starts by showing you what you fear, like last night."

"Have they ever done it? Have they taken people?" Elijah asked.

"Yes," R.L.'s eyes glazed over for a second like he was remembering. "But, people have also come back from it. People have resisted."

"How?" asked Adam.

The ringleader gave him a small smile. "By training, by being honest. By letting me know if you think they have gotten too far into your mind."

"What if they come back? What do we do?" Laura rubbed the mark on her arm subconsciously.

"Keep your eyes closed. Think of anything other than what they are trying to make you see and hear. Focus on good things. And lean on each other. Lean on your circus." R.L. patted her knee and then stood up. "For tonight, enjoy the party. Have fun and sleep well," he said before disappearing, leaving nothing but a cloud of glittery red smoke.

"Think he could teach us how to do that?" Jaiden said to the others.

"I still think we're dreaming." Adam stood up and put his hands in his pockets. "I mean, come on, this is crazy."

"I don't know. It's kinda cool," Elijah offered.

"Shut up, Eli," Adam snapped at him.

"Dude, what's your problem?" Stella jumped up and stood

only a few inches from his face. She had no tolerance for bullies.

"Not with you, so back off," Adam retorted.

"Hey," Jaiden pushed Adam back and stood in front of him. "We just heard a whole story of people going from normal to evil shadow creatures, and you really wanna be a jerk right now?"

Adam scoffed. "Whatever." He walked off into the crowd.

"How do you guys know each other?" Stella asked.

"We go to the same school." Elijah's face was hot with embarrassment.

"He bother you there too?" Stella demanded.

"It's not a big deal, okay?" Elijah tried to play it off. "Just leave it."

Jaiden cut Stella off before she could keep pressing, "come on, let's go look around."

"Fine," Stella and Laura linked arms and followed behind the boys. "That guy's such a jerk," she whispered to Laura who nodded in agreement.

ADAM LET the door to the Side Show close behind him as he walked down the hallway and into the Commons. He didn't want to be around anyone right now. They were all on Elijah's side, of course. Everyone always was. *Poor little Elijah.* He turned to start up the stairs to the Hall of Choice but then changed his mind. He looked around and weighed his options.

Once he was in the hallway that headed to the dining hall, he had to decide whether to go right or left. R.L. hadn't shown them either of the halls, so who knew where they led. *Eenie, meanie, miny, mo.* He turned right and walked slowly.

The walls were light brown, and the farther down the hallway Adam went, the older the walls looked. Cracks started appearing. The paint started to look chipped. There were maps hanging on both sides of him that appeared older the farther he walked. At the end of the hall was a tall brick archway. A thick mist floated inside it, calling him to walk through it.

Adam peered down the hallway to see if anyone was coming to get him. He waited a couple of minutes, and when it stayed empty, he stepped through. Recognition hit him like a slap in the face. He knew this room. He knew that worn yellow couch and hole in the wall behind it all too well. This was *his* living room. Just like the Shadow had shown him. Was this them? Were they trying to get him? Or did he somehow end up home? Did he just walk through the exit or something?

"Jenn!" Adam's eyes almost bugged out of his skull when an angry voice yelled his mom's name. He whipped his head all around, trying to find whoever was calling for his mom.

A man walked into the living room and looked right at Adam. "Jenn," the man said again. *He can't see me*, Adam realized. The man wasn't looking at him. He was looking through him.

Adam turned around and couldn't believe what he saw. It was his mom, but a way younger version. She had a baby on her hip. *Is that me?* Adam wondered.

"Yes?" she said to the man. She looked scared like she was ready to run.

Adam didn't pay attention to what the man was saying. All he could focus on was his mom. She had a bruise on her chin. Her hair was a mess. Her eyes were red, like she had been crying. She was bouncing the baby up and down.

"Let me just put Adam down first," Jenn said to the man. *So that is me.* He never imagined his mom holding him as a baby. It was a hard picture to get used to. He can't remember the last time she'd even hugged him.

"What did I just say?" Adam was pulled out of his thoughts when the man yelled.

Jenn backed up and held Adam close to her chest. She closed her eyes and flinched. The man started towards her, his hands balled up in fists.

"No!" Adam screamed without thinking. But the man didn't hear him and Adam couldn't grab onto him even though he tried. The man looked so angry. It was scary.

Then, someone appeared between Adam's mom and the man.

"R.L.?" Adam asked out loud.

The ringleader didn't hear him either. He stood with a challenging look in his eyes. The man stopped walking towards Jenn, and confusion replaced the anger on his face. R.L. didn't say anything, but it didn't seem like the man saw him. He was still focused on Jenn, but something had made him pause. He didn't seem to realize that R.L. had put a hand to his chest to stop him.

"Might want to get the door," R.L. said right before the doorbell rang.

The man stopped in his tracks. He looked between the door and Adam's mom. The bell kept ringing. The man mumbled under his breath and went to see who it was. Jenn took a shaky breath and held back a sob. Baby Adam began to fuss, and she rubbed his face and kissed the top of his head.

Adam watched R.L. watching his mom. *What the heck?*

"Don't worry, he's going out for a while," R.L. told Jenn. She didn't acknowledge him. She didn't know he was there.

"I'm going out," the man called before closing the door.

Adam looked at the ringleader. "How did you know that?" he tried asking him.

R.L. didn't respond. Instead, he watched as Jenn walked through the house to Adam's room. As soon as she walked into the bedroom, Adam was back in the brown hallway.

"Wait," Adam muttered. He started forward through the arch again but a voice surprised him.

"History." Barnaby turned his pocket watch over in his hands.

"What?" Adam panted. His heart was beating so hard he could hear it in his ears.

"You walked into history," Barnaby's voice was serious. "Something that happened in the past. Kind of like a memory."

"R.L. was there, in my house. When I was a baby and that man—" he didn't finish his sentence. He couldn't get the man's furious face out of his mind.

"Yes, he was. He helped that night. Could have been far worse," Barnaby said calmly. He could see the fear in Adam and the understanding. Even if Adam didn't want to admit it, he had an idea about who that angry man had been.

"So, R.L. knew me back then?" Adam's voice echoed through the hallway.

"Yes."

Adam waited for more, but Barnaby was silent.

"That's it? That's all you got to say?" Adam stepped towards the short man.

Barnaby tilted his head up and frowned. "Adam, R.L. has been there more than you will ever know. Moments that were bad could have been a lot worse if he hadn't stepped in. He has known you for a long time, has known your mother for a long time. What you just saw was one of the thousands of times he was there."

"I never saw him," Adam didn't care that his eyes were watering or that his lip was trembling. A movie reel of moments from his past was playing in his head, the worst of the worst. And all he kept thinking was, *R.L. was there.*

15. THE TRUTH

Training had continued the next morning after a fairly quiet breakfast. Adam was in no mood to talk, Stella was nervous about the horses, and Jaiden was so hungry he was stuffing his face. Elijah and Laura had casually chatted, recounting the events of the night before in the Side Show.

Now, standing with Julie, Stella was being educated on all things equestrian. Her anxiety was through the roof, even after Julie telling her that Domino would be able to sense it. *Breathe, just breathe,* she repeated to herself.

"Never walk up behind a horse. They spook easy," Julie told Stella.

"Really?" Stella stayed behind her instructor as they walked towards Domino from the side. There was a cool breeze that swayed the tall grass gently.

"Hey, Domino," Julie greeted the horse. "Yeah," she spoke to Stella, "they're prey animals. They're food. So their instincts are to run and fight." Domino ate an apple from Julie's hand. "They kick and bite what they can't see. So don't come up from behind, and if you're feeding him, always stretch your hand out and have your palm up so he doesn't accidentally bite off your fingers."

"Good to know," Stella hesitantly rubbed Domino's face. He moved his head towards her.

"He likes you," Julie said. "This is a halter." Julie gestured to the white rope ensemble on Domino's head. "We attach a lead rope to the bottom of it, under his chin, and it makes it easy to guide him."

"Where are we taking him?"

"Called a round pen. It's over a ways. You're gonna start riding today." Julie clipped the rope, and they started walking through the field.

"Um, I don't know. Don't you think it's a bit soon?" Stella argued.

Julie just looked at her.

"Seriously, Julie come on."

"Stella, you were made for this. Once you get started, it's gonna fall into place. Gotta trust me."

"Don't horses, like, throw you off?"

"Domino won't. Yours might," Julie said as if it wasn't a big deal.

"Well, what happens then? What happens when it throws me off, and I hit the ground?" Stella exclaimed.

Julie stopped walking, put one hand on Stella's shoulder, smiled, and said, "You get up."

"Baseball, huh?" Arlo asked. He slid on more weight as Jaiden laid on the bench.

"Yeah, I'm pretty good. Hoping to get scholarships in the future and stuff." Jaiden's arms ached. He had never been much of a weights guy. Arlo was still pretty dead set on stuffing him inside a cannon, despite Jaiden's logical arguments.

"I did some football back in my day, but I never really loved it. I eventually quit." Arlo spoke as he stood behind Jaiden's head and let his hands hover underneath the bar, just in case.

"Did you go to college?" Jaiden asked between presses.

"Failed out of school pretty early on. Wasn't for me."

"My dad would've killed me," Jaiden grunted.

"Keep your breathing steady," Arlo instructed. "Dad's big on school?"

"Yeah," Jaiden ground out. "Gotta make something of myself."

"Why?" Arlo asked.

"What?" Jaiden gave his instructor a confused look.

"Why?" Arlo repeated. "Why do you gotta make something of yourself? Why does he care so much right now? You got a lotta years ahead."

Jaiden thought about it for a few minutes. Arlo told him to take a break and helped him up. They sat down with some water, and Jaiden tried to figure out how to answer. He could hear his dad's voice in his head, *you have to get ahead while you're young. You might have a disadvantage, but you can't let that stop you. You have to be prepared for the future.*

"My parents," Jaiden began, "they came to this country, or well my home country, cause I'm not sure where the heck we actually are right now." Arlo laughed at that. "So that me and my sisters could have a better life than they did. I'm, uh, the oldest and the only boy, so they expect a lot. I have to make sure I have a successful future, can't let their sacrifices go to waste. I have to get good grades and do sports to hopefully get scholarships. Gotta make everyone proud, you know?"

"That's a lot," Arlo said.

"Yeah," Jaiden felt guilty thinking about his family. He's

left them all behind to what? Lift weights in a circus? Go to parties and bonfires? They're probably worried sick. *Let them worry,* he thought. *You deserve a break.* And those thoughts just made the guilt worse.

"I didn't come from much," Arlo took a sip of his water. "My mom wasn't around. She left when I was young. My dad worked hard but barely made enough for us to live. I didn't grow up in a nice neighborhood or nice house. My dad said similar stuff to me. Told me I had to make something of myself. Told me to do what I needed to do to make money."

"What did you end up doing?"

"I ended up here. R.L. saved me after I did something real stupid and real embarrassing. He gave me a chance. This mark," he clutched his forearm in his hand. "This mark made me something, something better than I ever coulda made." He smiled.

Jaiden thought that over.

"Now come on, rookie, back to work." Arlo stood up and snickered at Jaiden's groans and complaints.

LAURA STUCK her tongue out of her lips ever so slightly as she concentrated on attempting to juggle. *1, 2, 3. 1, 2, 3.* She tried counting to keep in rhythm with the plush balls she was throwing, but she had no luck. She dropped one every time.

"Ugh!" she yelled.

"Okay, okay," Etta soothed. "So, juggling is not your thing. No biggie, we'll find what is."

"Yeah," Amos picked up four bowling pins and tossed them around and around effortlessly with a smug smile. "No biggie."

"Good for you," Laura mocked before throwing one of

the balls at him. He dropped all the pins, and she laughed harder than she thought she would. She turned to Etta who was staring at her with something in her eyes. "What?" "Come on. I think I know just what your thing is." Etta grabbed her hand and led her through Clown Alley.

"SEE? YOU GUYS ARE NATURALS," Hank encouraged.

Adam and Eli brought their legs back to the ground after finally succeeding at a handstand. Adam was angry and embarrassed about how long it took, especially after Eli had done it before him. *Show off*, Adam thought.

"Yeah, this might not be so bad," Eli said.

"I'll get you guys some water," Hank told them.

Maybe I should try talking to him, Elijah thought when he looked at Adam. They hadn't spoken except for a few under the breath comments and Adam telling him to shut up. *If we're gonna have to work together, we might as well try to be cool.*

"This is weird, huh? Training to be in a circus?" Elijah said.

"Shut up, Eli," was Adam's response.

"Look," Elijah put his hands up and took a step back. "I'm just trying to be nice."

Adam closed the distance between them and pushed him backward, hard. "I don't want you to be nice! I don't *need* you to be nice!" He pushed Elijah again.

"Okay, okay!" Elijah continued to walk backward but Adam kept coming.

"Just 'cause we're stuck together right now doesn't mean I like you and doesn't mean I need anything from you!" He pushed Elijah one last time before being pulled away. Adam looked to see a very angry Hank standing between them.

"Absolutely, not," Hank told him. He looked at Elijah and asked, "are you okay?"

Elijah's hands were shaking. He was embarrassed, and he was mad. Cirque was supposed to be an escape from the real world, and it was, except for Adam always having to ruin it.

Adam lost it. He stepped forward, yelling, "Sure, ask if he's okay. Wouldn't want the poor little baby to be hurt!"

"Adam," Hank tried to reason but was cut off by Elijah yelling back.

"What's your problem? What's wrong with you? I've never done anything to you!"

Hank stood in between the boys to keep them from tackling each other.

"You're my problem," Adam shouted. "You make everyone feel sorry for you just 'cause something bad happened to you!"

"My dad died!" Elijah cried in bewilderment.

"So what? Lots of people grow up without dads! No one ever gave me a break! Why do you deserve one?" Adam panted. His chest heaved up and down. He clenched and unclenched his fists.

Elijah was silent. The other acrobats stood still. Cirque performers who had been practicing in the area didn't move a muscle. Hank looked at Adam, his heart breaking. Adam didn't even realize he was crying. All he felt was anger, especially now that Elijah looked at him like he pitied him.

"At least your dad is dead," Adam said quietly. Elijah sobbed, a pain shooting through his chest. "And he didn't just leave 'cause he didn't want you." The anger started to turn to a feeling Adam never could name. All he knew was it made him feel like a little kid waiting in a house, looking at a door, deep down knowing his dad would never walk through it again.

The face of the angry man he had seen the night before flashed in his mind, making him feel even worse. He couldn't remember what his dad even looked like. His mom didn't have any pictures. But he knew, he knew, that the man he had seen through the door of History was his father.

"I'm sorry," Elijah whispered. Adam looked at him, confused. "I'm sorry your dad left, but I do know how you feel. My dad is gone too. Maybe different reasons why, but I still don't have one. Just like you. I don't like people treating me any different. I hate it. Just makes everything more real."

Makes sense, Adam thought. He wasn't gonna say anything, though. This was already too much.

"Holding everything in," Hank said, looking at each boy. "Is one of the most exhausting things in the world. Maybe it's not normal for you to say how you're feeling or what you're thinking, but it's healthy. It's the right thing to do. Try and do it more often, yeah?"

"Yeah," Elijah mumbled.

I do feel kinda better, Adam confessed to himself.

"Come on," They followed Hank through Cirque and ended up in the kitchen. They sat on stools at a giant counter island, Hank between the boys. The floor was black and white checkered like a vintage diner and the smell of cookies made all three guys' mouths water.

"Hey there," a woman with red hair greeted. She spoke with a thick Irish accent.

"Boys, this is Amelia," said Hank. "Amelia, this is Elijah and Adam. We had a tough training today. Got anything good?"

Amelia clapped her hands together excitedly, "I have just

the thing!" Elijah smiled, amused by her giggle and how she moved clumsily around the kitchen.

"Acrobats need to carbo-load. Gotta eat more than usual to stay strong," Hank said. They sat in silence for a minute until Hank began speaking again. "I used to push everyone away. I was pissed at the world, cause nothing ever worked out for me. I felt like I had to work harder at everything and still didn't catch any breaks. And the angrier I got at the world, the angrier I got at myself and almost any person I met. But, you know what made me change?"

They shook their heads.

"To be an acrobat, to try and get my head on straight, I had to work with other people. I had to trust other people. When you're being thrown in the air or standing on each other's shoulders, you have to trust each other. You have to let strangers, or enemies, become friends. It takes work from everyone. But it's worth it."

"Here you are," Amelia set a plate filled with cookies and brownies on the counter. She gave them each a small plate and a cup of milk.

"My mom hates me," Adam said after feeling a burst of courage. He had never told anyone anything about his mom. He stared at the cookie in his hand and then looked at the guys.

Elijah's eyebrows furrowed, *how could a mom hate her kid?*

"Why do you say that?" Hank asked.

"She says it," Adam laughed humorlessly. "She hates me. She pushes me around some. We don't have a lot of money, so I don't have a phone or nice clothes or anything. I think I'm jealous of you," he told Elijah. *Guess this circus makes you honest,* Adam snorted at the thought.

"You scare me," Elijah repaid his honesty. Adam creased

his eyebrows in thought. He had a brief sickening feeling at the thought of scaring someone like his dad had scared his mom. "But it also makes me angry because I wish I was tough, like you. Then maybe things wouldn't hurt so much. Me and my mom are cool, but she doesn't like talking about my dad."

Adam nodded his head. Elijah gave him a small smile.

Hank gulped down his milk, "I'm not saying you have to be best friends. But we are family here. And you do have to trust each other when we train and perform, or we could all get hurt. Okay?"

"Okay," the boys said at the same time.

"Cool," Hank nodded and smiled. "Wow, I am acing this whole training thing." That made the boys chuckle and earned a loud laugh from Amelia, who stood over a pot on the other side of the kitchen. "I hope that wasn't a sarcastic laugh," Hank grunted.

Amelia turned and winked. "No, not at all."

16. THE FESTIVAL

"So, this festival," Stella said, "what's it called again?" She walked beside Barnaby, who stopped in front of a door that no one even realized was there. It had blended in with the wall at the end of the hallway they were in.

R.L. had told them that after breakfast, Barnaby would take them to a festival in Ekklesia. It would be a rest from training and a chance to explore the city.

"This place has too many doors and hallways," Jaiden whispered to Laura and Elijah, who nodded in agreement.

Adam was a few feet behind the group, walking slowly. He couldn't stop thinking about the night he walked through the History door. He couldn't get his mom's face out of his head. He couldn't stop replaying the moment R.L. appeared and stopped the man from whatever he was about to do. He also felt stupid and embarrassed for being so honest with Hank and Elijah. *I should've kept my mouth shut.*

"The Orsus festival is one of Ekklesia's yearly

celebrations. We celebrate beginnings," Barnaby turned the knob and pushed the door open.

"Beginnings?" Elijah's question went unanswered when the city of Ekklesia came into view.

A beautiful, energetic city sparkled in the brilliant sunlight. The sky was a perfect blue with a few white puffy clouds. The sidewalks were so clean you could eat off them, and the road was so perfectly paved and smooth it looked fake.

"Welcome to Ekklesia," Barnaby smiled proudly at his city.

The group began to walk down the streets. Every head was tilted back to be able to see all the different buildings. None of the kids had ever seen any kind of city like this. Big houses with front porches sat right next to red brick apartment buildings. There were huge castle-type buildings that each took up half of a block, with clocks on the towers and tall windows. Right next to those were tall high-rise buildings reflective on every side, stretching high into the sky.

The streets were flooded with people of every race. Everyone was smiling and laughing like they all knew each other. Live music and shouts from vendors filled the city; fruit stands, hot dog carts, ice cream trucks, markets.

"Where are we?" Laura asked Barnaby. They passed a picturesque park filled with people having picnics and playing sports.

"Ekklesia." Laura rolled her eyes at Barnaby's answer. She should've expected a lack of details. He and R.L. were good at that.

Adam's thoughts of his mom and his own vulnerability were silenced as he took in Ekklesia. It was perfect, like actually perfect. *But that's not possible,* he internally argued. *There was no city in the world that was perfect. Maybe Barnaby was messing with them and took them through some weird door like I walked through last night.*

"Hey Barnaby," Adam jogged ahead to walk beside the man, "is this place for real?"

"Real as in, does this place actually exist? Are you actually walking in an actual city?" Barnaby retorted.

Adam just stared at him, causing Barnaby to laugh.

"It's just." Adam looked around. "There's no way everything is this good. Like how are the sidewalks and streets so perfect? There's no trash anywhere. Everyone's chillin' and, I don't know. Just doesn't seem possible."

Barnaby stopped walking and faced the group. They all stopped and waited for whatever he was going to say. Barnaby smiled, "After everything that you've seen and experienced so far, a city that people keep clean, a city where everyone loves and respects each other, is the thing that seems the most impossible?"

The group processed that. They had seen their friends and family disappear on a carousel and ended up in a circus with magical tattoos made of moonlight. They had been attacked by Shadows, seen a campfire change colors, and been around people in the Side Show with scales, fur, multiple legs and more strange qualities.

"You have a point," Adam figured. He shook his head, still in disbelief.

"It saddens me that it is a rarity to find a city that people call home in such good shape. And it saddens me even more that it is a rarity to find a city where people treat each other as people." Barnaby frowned.

"The world sucks." Stella deadpanned. The others nodded in agreement.

Barnaby snickered, "Usually. Come on, this way."

They walked past the park and stopped near a huge stone fountain. There was a statue inside of a man reaching down and helping someone up. There were no features on either of the figures, but Elijah's first thought was that the man reaching down reminded him of R.L.

"The festival is starting soon, but before it does R.L. wanted to give you a good view of Ekklesia. He should be here any moment now." Barnaby told them. Laura sat on the fountain and looked inside. It was filled with coins.

"What happens during the festival?" Jaiden asked.

"So many things! Fireworks, amazing food, singing, painting-" Barnaby was cut off by the ringleader.

"Costumes and dancing and lights." R.L. put his arm around his friend.

"It's surely something to witness," Barnaby added.

"But first." R.L. Adjusted the top hat he was wearing. "A bird's eye view of our splendid city."

TEN MINUTES LATER, a red and white striped hot air balloon was lifting them above the city. It took some coaxing to get Elijah and Stella on, and they didn't dare go near the edge.

"This can't be safe," Stella whispered to Elijah. They huddled together in the middle while everyone else looked down.

"There's too many of us in here," Elijah stressed. *I think I'm gonna barf.*

R.L. looked at them with amusement.

"This isn't funny," Stella snapped.

R.L. walked over to them. "You're right. I'm very sorry. But, have I lied to you yet?"

Elijah and Stella just looked at each other.

"Correct, I have not," R.L. continued. "I promise you. You are as safe here as you are on the ground. And you will regret not seeing all Ekklesia has to offer. It is more than just the city that you saw."

Stella and Elijah looked over at Laura when she gasped at the view.

"I promise." R.L. offered each of them a hand.

"Fine, but if I die." Stella gripped his hand and Elijah did the same.

"Then you can tell me 'I told you so.'" The ringleader led them to the edge.

They inched their way forward and had to admit that R.L. was right, as he usually seemed to be. They would have regretted not seeing this.

A red and white circus tent sat in the middle of the city where they had just been. R.L. explained that that was Cirque.

"It's huge," Jaiden gasped. "No wonder there's so many hallways."

Waves crashed onto white shores, just north of the city. An ocean, bluer than blue, spread endlessly in front of them. Jaiden turned his head and saw a jungle. The looks of the trees reminded him of R.L.'s tattoos. He spotted the ringleader. His tattoos were in full view under the black T-shirt he wore. Jaiden could see animals moving within the jungle on his arm, just like the jungle ahead of him.

"How?" Adam asked. He stood next to Barnaby. They stared into a golden desert and watched camels carrying travelers. And huge mountains covered in snow seemed to be right next to the desert, but in their own realm all at the same time, just like the beach and the jungle.

Barnaby gave him a look, and Adam knew there were no answers he could give that would satisfy him, just like R.L. had said before. "It just is," Barnaby said. And Adam decided that his answer was enough.

"Okay," Adam whispered. "Hey." Barnaby looked at him. "That door, if I go back through it, will I see more history moments? Times when R.L. was there."

Barnaby thought for a moment before answering, "Yes, you will. But, you can also ask R.L. about it. He'll answer your questions."

"I don't know. You guys aren't very good at that," Adam teased.

Barnaby bellowed a laugh, Adam smiled at him.

"This is beautiful." Laura felt like she could stare at the ocean for hours.

"It really is. Better than our city," Jaiden said.

"Yeah, seriously." Laura was quiet for a minute and then spoke low so no one else could hear, "Do you miss home?"

"Honestly? I don't know," he answered. He had been thinking about it. The last few days had been intense and weird but also fun. There hadn't been pressure, besides the cannonball thing, which he was still trying to find a way out of. He continued, "At home, I always feel like I'm under pressure. Like I gotta do everything right to make my parents happy, to make them look good and stuff. Here, I just, I get to do what I want. I get to ask questions and have an opinion, and figure it out. I don't know, maybe that doesn't make sense," he started to trail off.

"No, no, I get you," Laura assured him. "I kinda don't want to go home. All home is for me is my parents fighting and me having to be in the middle of it all the time. I constantly feel like I have to choose one over the other. It's exhausting. I'm just so tired of it. But, this, I mean wow." They stared below them in silence for a moment. "Even though I am marked as a clown." She and Jaiden laughed. "It's better than home."

"Amen to that," Stella said. Jaiden and Laura looked over at her in surprise. "You guys are kinda loud. You realize we're all like right next to each other on a balloon, right?"

"You don't want to go home either?" Laura laughed as she asked.

"I'm torn. I feel bad leaving my grandma and cousins hanging, but," she looked around her, "this is pretty dope. And I don't have to be so responsible. At home, I have to do a lot. Help out a lot. Here, I can–"

"Just be," Jaiden finished for her. Stella nodded.

"What about you guys?" Stella asked loud enough for Elijah and Adam to hear. "You guys miss home?" Barnaby and R.L. raised their eyebrows at the question.

"I miss my mom," Elijah told her. "But, I'd rather be here than there."

Stella nodded and looked at Adam. After a few seconds, she rolled her eyes. *The jerk never talks,* she thought.

"No," Adam answered but didn't look at anyone while speaking. He just stared at the mountains. "Home sucks. I definitely don't miss it."

Stella was shocked that he had said so much. The balloon began to make its descent back towards the city. The music had picked up, and it looked like there were people in colorful costumes dancing around.

"I'm very glad you're all here." They all looked at the ringleader as he spoke. "Home is very different for all of you, and I hope that maybe you'll consider Cirque and Ekklesia your second home."

"That's like your third hot dog!" Stella laughed as Jaiden stuffed his face and shrugged his shoulders. She continued to eat her cotton candy, and they watched the Cirque contortionists and acrobats do tricks for a crowd that had gathered.

It was dark now, and the Orsus festival was in full swing. All of the buildings were lit up with different colored lights. Different bands were taking turns playing all genres of music. People in colorful costumes of feathers and beads were dancing in the streets.

"Hey," a boy from the Side Show covered in hair greeted Jaiden and Stella.

"Hey," they said in unison.

"I'm Logan or the dog boy," he smiled and handed them a sparkler.

"We'll stick to Logan," Stella said.

"Orsus is the best time of the year. Can I hang out with you guys?" Logan asked.

"Yeah," Jaiden nodded.

Laura had joined some of the artists and was painting on a canvas they had strung up on the side of the building. Her hands were covered in colors and her cheeks had white stars painted on them by a little boy who was currently drawing on a sidewalk with chalk.

Adam and Barnaby were trying samples from every food stall. Adam had never even heard of some of the types of food they had. Spicy and sweet, and everything in between was represented. He usually didn't experiment with meals, but Barnaby had dared him, and he wasn't one to say no to a dare.

"How do they not melt?" Elijah asked R.L. They stood in front of a towering ice sculpture of the Cirque tent.

"Magic?" R.L. quipped. Elijah gave the ringleader a look that made him laugh.

"The same magic that makes your tattoos move?" Elijah questioned.

"Or not magic," R.L. said with a wink and a smile.

They walked over to the next ice sculpture. This one was of a man wearing a top hat. One hand held the rim of his hat while the other rested on a cane in front of him. His arms were muscular, and he had shoulder-length hair.

"That's you," Elijah said.

"Appears so," R.L. squinted his eyes and looked hard at the sculpture. "Although," he said quietly and leaned his head down near Elijah like he was telling him a secret. "They didn't get my arms quite right. My biceps are definitely bigger than that."

Elijah laughed as they walked over to Jaiden and Stella. Barnaby and Adam joined them shortly after.

"Excuse me for a moment," R.L. walked towards the main stage that was situated near the fountain.

"Hey guys," Laura sat next to Stella on the ground.

"This is Logan," Jaiden introduced them to the dog boy.

"Have fun?" Stella asked Laura.

"So much, I haven't painted in so long. You should look later," she told the group.

"Ladies and gentlemen!" R.L.'s voice hushed the crowd. The music lowered, and all eyes were on him. "Citizens of Ekklesia! We are here to celebrate another wonderful Orsus!"

The kids clapped along with everyone else. Even Adam let out a shout. Jaiden and Eli looked at each other in shock. *We'll see how long this good mood lasts,* Elijah said to himself.

"Orsus means beginning. It means undertaking. It means initiative. That is what we do every day. We choose to begin. We choose to continue with seemingly impossible undertakings. And we choose to take initiative, to make a difference. You make Ekklesia what it is. You make Cirque what it is. And though we've had our bouts with darkness, even recently." Laura's skin crawled at the thought of the Shadows. "We persist, we overcome, and we stand. So! My stupendous city and remarkable family" –R.L. took off his top hat and raised it in the air– "here's to you!"

Fireworks exploded in the sky. A rainbow of colors splayed across the dark above Ekklesia. Firecrackers were set off in the streets. The dog boy howled making the group laugh. Sparklers were bright in people's hands. Canons of colorful powder decorated the crowd. The band belted out a song about their city. And five kids realized that there was a world a lot bigger than the one they thought they knew.

17. THE CHANCE

"And then, kick the hat each time you step forward, like this," Amos stepped towards the top hat that was on the ground and kicked it further away from him.

"And people find it funny?" Laura asked him.

"Well, you gotta play the part. You gotta have fun with it. And then you can show off a bit." Amos went to the hat and stepped on its rim causing it to bounce in the air. He kicked it higher and higher into the air until it landed on his head. "Tada," he bowed and Laura giggled. "See? That's why I love my mark. We get to make people laugh."

"I guess," Laura murmured. She still wasn't convinced that this whole clown thing was for her.

"The sooner you give your mark a chance, the sooner you'll realize why you were marked with it in the first place," Amos remarked.

"What do you mean?" Laura questioned.

"We're marked with what we're marked with for a reason.

You'll figure it out soon," he didn't seem like he was going to elaborate.

Laura just stared at the ink on her skin. *Why would I be marked as a clown? Am I meant to make other people laugh? Meant to make a fool out of myself? Maybe it's a lesson in not caring what other people think?* She pondered the possibilities until Amos got her attention again.

"You should be excited. We get to come up with a whole new act for you. It's fun! We get to brainstorm and try different things and make some up as we go." He handed her a pink tube.

"What is this?" she asked.

"Bubbles."

"Fascinating." Laura's bored tone made Amos chuckle.

She opened the tube and started blowing the bubbles. She gasped as they morphed into different shapes the size of her head. Lions, horses, a carousel, a clown. She looked at Amos for an explanation.

"Bubbles," he mimicked her flat tone and winked.

"I think I know the perfect act," Etta announced. The kids jumped in surprise. She pushed herself off of the wall she had been leaning against.

"How long have you been there?" Amos went ignored as Etta continued.

"Are you afraid of heights?" Etta asked Laura.

"I'm afraid to answer that question," she quipped in response.

Etta just laughed and smiled a smile that could only mean she had a crazy scheme up her sleeve.

· · ·

STELLA LOOKED over the herd of horses, waiting for one of them to speak to her. That's how Julie described finding your horse that he or she would speak to you. Stella had rolled her eyes, of course, but decided to listen to her instructor anyway.

Riding Domino had started rocky (it was all Stella's doing though, Domino was perfectly behaved) but once Stella had gotten used to it, she loved it. It felt like she was flying. The wind hitting her face and the sound of Domino's hooves on the ground were better than she could have imagined.

Her eyes continued to scan over the valley when she felt her heart leap in her chest out of nowhere. A beautiful golden horse with a white mane and tail ran down the hill towards the other horses. Its loud neigh made Stella smile.

"And that would be the one," Julie commented.

Stella kept her eyes on the horse as Julie walked towards them, put a halter on its head, and attached the lead rope. The horse didn't seem too happy to follow Julie's lead, but she corrected it and walked to the round pen, a wooden fence encircling a large area of grass.

"This girl is beautiful, great choice," Julie told Stella.

"What's her name?" Stella asked.

"That's up to you," Julie told her. She started giving some instructions to the horse and having her run in circles in the round pen.

Stella smiled at the sounds coming from the horse like she was annoyed that Julie was telling her what to do. *Same,* she thought.

"Nova," Stella whispered to herself. She remembered hearing the word before. Whether it was in school or on TV, she couldn't recall. But she knew it was a type of star and that it was without a doubt the name of this horse. "Nova," she announced to Julie.

Julie nodded her head, "Fitting. Alright, let's get to work."

❖

Julie had brought Stella to stand beside her as they worked with Nova. They stood in the middle of the pen as Nova ran around them close to the fence. For the first hour, Nova was not having it. She would buck her body as she ran, wouldn't make eye contact with her trainers, and didn't want them near her.

But Julie had a talent with training, and soon Nova was more responsive. So much so that Julie even got a saddle on her and rode her. Nova bucked and tried to throw Julie off, but Julie hung tight. Stella's eyes were about to bust out of her head when Nova started going crazy. She couldn't believe how Julie could stay on. Once Nova settled down, she trotted and even galloped around the pen with Julie on her back.

"Whoa," Julie said to Nova. She came to a stop, and Julie got off and stood beside Stella.

"Your turn," Julie told her.

"What? No way." Stella took a few steps back and shook her head.

"Stella–"

"She almost threw you off! What if she does it to me too? I'm not experienced enough. This is too soon," she tried to reason.

"You were made for this. Nova is yours, meant for you. You'll see, you're going to be a natural." Julie's voice was soft and patient. She walked over to a bin that sat outside of the pen and got a black helmet out. She handed it to Stella, but she shook her head.

"No." Her heart pounded in her chest.

"Stella breathe," Julie repeated for the fifth time since they started.

"I'm breathing," Stella responded tightly. All she could think about was how bad it would hurt if Nova freaked out and threw her off, and she hit the ground.

"What are you afraid of?"

Stella thought it was pretty obvious, "Falling and it hurting, duh."

Julie nodded her head and was silent in thought for a moment. Then she said, "The first time I rode Domino, he was not having it. He hadn't been trained yet, but I knew he was supposed to be mine. When my trainer brought me out here, like I brought you, Domino called to me" –she rubbed Nova's neck– "he was good to me, except for when it was time to train."

"He threw me off a few times, and yeah, it hurt." Julie connected her eyes with her trainee's. "But I'm going to tell you, just like my instructor told me. You have to get back up. You have to show that you're not giving up. When Domino realized that, he stopped fighting me and we were able to work together. Just like I did with Nova earlier."

"Didn't it hurt? Hitting the ground? Weren't you terrified he would stomp you or bite you?" Stella exclaimed.

"Yes, it hurt, and I had moments of fear, but all I kept thinking about was how I wanted to experience the freedom that Domino could give me." They were silent for a few minutes. "I think, the bottom line is that you don't trust Nova, and you don't trust me," Julie stated matter of factly.

Stella looked down at the ground. She whispered, "I mean, I do a little, you more than her."

"We can't do this if you don't trust me," Julie insisted gently.

The only person I really trust is Grandma, Stella thought. Suddenly she saw her mom. Standing at the front door, the desperate look in her eyes, and then doing what she always did—walking away.

"I had a hard time trusting too," Julie confessed. "My dad hurt my mom and me when I was growing up. It made me not want to lean on anyone."

Stella looked at her in surprise.

"But then R.L. told me something when I met him," Julie smiled fondly. "He said, 'pain is inescapable.' He explained how we couldn't live this life without being hurt or betrayed, or sad. It's going to come whether we're all alone or surrounded by others. We can choose not to trust and try to deal with pain on our own. Or, we can take a chance on people and let them help us when pain comes."

"People leave," the words left Stella's lips before she thought about them. Her voice sounded so small. She hated it.

"Yes, they do."

"Inspiring," Stella huffed.

Julie put a hand on Stella's shoulder, causing her to look up. "But some people stay, Stella. There are people who want to be in your life, some you've met, and some you haven't yet. You could miss out on a lot of things in this life if you don't give people and experiences a chance."

She might be right, Stella thought. She didn't have anyone back home except her family. But here, Cirque, they barely knew her, but they've shown her a side of people that she's never seen.

"That makes sense," she sighed.

"Just give me a chance," Julie pleaded. "Trust me, please. Trust Nova."

Stella closed her eyes, instantly regretting it when an image of her mom flooded her mind. Instead, she opened her eyes and looked at the woman in front of her. The only woman besides her family that was making an effort in her life. She looked at Nova, who bobbed her head toward Stella. She reached out cautiously to the horse and rubbed her forehead.

"Okay," Stella cleared her throat. "Okay," she said again, but this time with assurance and determination in her voice.

Julie smiled as Stella put the helmet on and fastened it. Stella put her foot in the saddle's stirrup and swung her leg over to sit on Nova. She straightened her posture and loosely gripped the horn of the saddle. Julie began to lead them around the pen.

Stella followed instructions on how to move with Nova as she began to speed up. Her heart was hammering in her chest as Nova galloped around and around. She didn't even realize how much fun she was having, but her laughter carried through the valley.

"Fantastic!" Hank called out to Adam and Elijah. The boys were panting and wiping the sweat off their foreheads as they laid on the blue tumbling mat.

"Longest hour of my life," Adam whined.

"Can you believe this is just a warm-up?" Elijah had never been so active in his life.

Hank walked over to them, smiling from ear to ear, finding them hysterical. "It seems like just yesterday I was you guys. Near collapsing on the floor," he said. "But you'll see, it'll get easier."

Adam had to admit, the training today had been kind of fun. They had been climbing and swinging on a huge jungle gym-type structure set up in some room down one of the million hallways in the circus.

"Okay, one of our last warm-ups for the day," Hank announced. "Handstands."

"Cool," Elijah said as they stood up. *Handstand, easy.*

"On a partner," Hank said. The boys looked at him like he had three heads.

"I don't think we're ready for that." Elijah looked at Adam and then back at his instructor pleadingly. *Adam's just gonna drop me, and if I drop him I'm dead,* Elijah stressed in his head.

"You are, trust me." Hank smiled. "So Adam, you're gonna lift Elijah."

"Um." Adam shook his head. He looked at Elijah. *There's no way he's gonna let me do this. He has no reason to trust me,* Adam thought. Guilt about how he had treated Elijah made him look at the floor.

Elijah took a deep breath and said, "I trust you."

Adam's head whipped up towards Elijah, "What?"

"I trust you," he repeated slowly. Convincing himself it was true. Maybe he didn't trust him completely, but if they could do this handstand, he would.

"Alright." Hank clapped his hands. "Here's how we do it. Elijah, stand in front of Adam with your back facing him. Adam, you're gonna grab his hands like this." Hank demonstrated as he explained.

"Ready?" Adam asked after they had been coached.

"Yeah," Elijah said, trying to sound sure of himself.

Adam grabbed Elijah's hands, crouched down, and counted to three. On three, Elijah jumped up. Adam lifted him in the air, and Elijah landed with his feet on Adam's shoulders.

Both of their mouths hung open in shock. Did they really just do that?

"Yes!" Hank shouted. He stood next to the boys, ready to catch Elijah if anything went wrong. "Now, you're going to do what we talked about. Elijah, you're going to kick up and then straighten your legs. Adam, hold steady."

Other acrobats were watching the new recruits as they successfully pulled off their first partner handstand. Everyone clapped and hollered. The boys smiled. They couldn't believe they had pulled it off. And then, as quick as Elijah was up, he was falling down. Hank caught him swiftly and set him on the ground.

"I'm so sorry. My arms just started to shake," Adam explained quickly.

"It's okay. It's okay. I'm good," Elijah assured him. He laughed, still not able to believe they had actually done it.

"Excellent for your first try! You guys were meant for this. You're going to get better at it sooner than you realize." Hank hugged them both and Adam and Elijah shook hands.

"Thanks for not dropping me," Elijah said.

"Yeah," Adam smiled. "Hey uh, I'm sorry, for everything." He scratched the back of his head and looked everywhere except for the person he was apologizing to.

"Thanks," Elijah told him.

18. THE GLASS DESIRE

"Hey," Laura said. She sat down on a couch in the commons next to Stella. The three boys were sitting on a rug on the floor playing a card game. The fireplace was roaring, and soft music was playing somewhere in the room.

"I'm stuffed," Stella groaned. She closed her eyes, so close to falling asleep. Dinner had been too good to stop eating.

"We've mostly been weight lifting, but today he had me jump from one of the trapeze platforms to land in the net. To try to get me not to be scared and stuff," Jaiden told the boys after Elijah had asked about his training.

"And?" Stella questioned, opening one eye to see his facial expression.

"Still freaking terrified," Jaiden laughed nervously.

"I would be, too," Elijah said.

"You're all doing marvelously," R.L.'s voice came from behind the kids. They looked over as he stood next to the couch. "Your trainers have all told me amazing things."

"I can't tell if you're joking," Stella quipped. R.L. laughed.

"R.L.?" The group looked to Laura as she pulled a thick book from the bottom shelf of the coffee table in front of them. "What's this?" The dark red leather had intrigued her. It looked like a photo album.

She ran her hands over the smooth cover and spine. The aged leather groaned as Laura opened it and realized she was right. There were pictures of different groups of people all smiling and standing in front of the familiar red and white stripes of the circus tent. And R.L. was in every picture.

"Were these people at Cirque?" Elijah asked as he observed over Laura's shoulder.

Stella leaned over to see the photos and Jaiden put down the playing cards to join them in looking.

"Ah, yes." R.L. smiled warmly, his eyes softened like he stepped into a good memory.

"So many people," Laura whispered. She flipped through the pages. Under each photo were names scribbled underneath. She got towards the end of it and realized there were still some empty spots for pictures to be put. The last photo added was a group of teenagers. Laura ran her finger over the names and whispered them aloud.

Zoe, Jordan, Lilly, Drew, Michael

"So, they came here like us?" Jaiden questioned.

"They came here in a different way but for the same reasons. To find themselves, to find each other, to learn," R.L. answered. He laughed quietly to himself as if remembering something funny the group had done or said. "They were quite an interesting troupe."

"How many people have come here?" Adam hadn't moved

from where he was sitting but he was just as curious as the others.

"Many, many, many." R.L. reached for the album and rested his hand on the picture for a few seconds. "And many more will come. Now, why don't you all take to exploring?"

"Exploring?" Laura repeated.

"Anywhere you like," said R.L.

"How about that hallway?" Elijah said. "We could check out those doors."

"Not the scary one," Stella said.

"No way," Adam agreed.

"Good choice." R.L. winked.

THE KIDS STOOD in the Hall of Choice arguing over which door to go through.

"What did he say this door was again?" Stella asked, pointing to the ornate golden door.

"Lost room? Desire?" Elijah guessed.

"No, I think this is the lost room," Laura said as she stood next to the big wooden door.

"You guys are taking forever to decide," grumbled Adam.

"Like picking out what to watch on Netflix," Laura joked.

"Alright, I'm picking," Jaiden announced.

"Who put you in charge?" demanded Stella.

Jaiden ignored her and opened the Door of Desire.

"Fine, that's the door I was gonna say anyway," Stella huffed. She followed him through the door, the rest of the group behind her.

"Um." Laura glanced around. It looked like they were in a mall. A fancy and sparkling clean mall. *Not at all like the mall at home.*

"Interesting," said Jaiden. He jumped back when he turned and saw the group. "What the–"

"What?" Adam asked, only it wasn't Adam. It was an older guy with a beard wearing a suit. "Bro," the old-looking Adam said. "You look old." Jaiden was a full-grown man with some gray in his hair.

"Me? You look old!" Jaiden exclaimed, pointing at the aged face in front of him.

"Do I?" Laura asked. Everyone nodded.

"Safe to say, we all look old?" Stella asked.

The group responded with 'yeah's.'

Stella looked down at her hands but they looked the same as they did before they walked through the door. They turned and saw a storefront window. As she got closer, she could see her reflection–she looked exactly as she remembered. Stella called out, "Guys, come here."

The rest joined her and stared at their reflection in the window. The kids all still looked like kids to themselves, but when they looked at each other, they were twenty years older.

"So weird," Adam murmured.

"I wonder why—" Jaiden touched his face as his voice trailed off.

"What now?" Elijah asked.

"Might as well look around," Stella suggested.

They started walking through the mall. They looked in the different stores and then realized that they weren't stores at all. Through one store window, it looked like a bustling office. There were people in business clothes walking around, talking on phones and to each other. Adam felt a tug, something pulling him in there.

"I think I'm supposed to go in there," he told the group.

"Why?" Laura asked.

"I don't know" –he headed towards it– "just do. See ya later."

"What kind of mall is this?" Stella looked up to see level after level above her.

"Obviously, not a mall," Jaiden replied.

"Duh." Stella rolled her eyes.

"What do I look like?" Elijah asked Laura.

Laura gave Elijah a once over. "Your hair is a little longer. You have some wrinkles next to your eyes. Short beard. And your outfit kinda looks like something my science teacher would wear."

Elijah laughed and said, "You look like an art teacher."

Laura seemed pleased with that.

"How about me?" Stella turned around and asked them.

"You look like a mom of 5," Jaiden answered.

She punched him in the arm. "You look like you live in your parents' basement."

"I doubt that," Jaiden challenged. He looked at Laura and Elijah expecting a description of his appearance.

"Less basement, more lawyer," Laura smiled.

"You have a lot of gray hair," Elijah pointed out. Jaiden didn't seem too happy about that. He rubbed his head self-consciously.

"I think that's my spot," Stella announced. Through the glass, she saw the inside of a house and something told her that's where she had to go.

"Be careful," Laura cautioned.

"Up ahead, I think that's mine," Jaiden said.

"I'm gonna go up the escalator," Laura told the guys.

"I'll walk further down," Elijah decided.

. . .

"Sir, I have the reports you asked for." A man handed Adam a stack of papers.

"Huh?" Adam said.

The man seemed nervous. "The reports you, you asked for yesterday in the meeting? They're all there."

Adam just nodded his head and thanked the man. He spotted a door with his name next to it. He walked through it and into an office with a huge window overlooking a city.

"Huh," he breathed. "My own office." He sat at the desk chair and put his feet up. "Cool."

JAIDEN WALKED into what looked like a courthouse. There were some people in handcuffs and who he assumed were lawyers standing next to them. He looked down and realized he was suddenly holding a briefcase. *Lawyer? Nice. Is this some sort of glimpse into the future? Would this really happen one day?* His parents were probably thrilled that this was his job.

He walked down the hallway, saying, "Hi" to people who greeted him. Something in his pocket vibrated. He pulled out a phone with a name he didn't recognize, staring back at him.

"Hello?" he answered.

"Hey, just a reminder that your 3 o'clock got moved to 4 o'clock," the female voice rushed out.

"Okay, cool," Jaiden replied. The lady hung up immediately. He started to put his phone in his pocket when it started vibrating again. As soon as he answered the call, another woman started speaking.

"Your son has decided that he hates us," she said. *Son?*

"Uh, why?" Jaiden asked, playing along.

"Because of the date thing," she said as if he should know what she's talking about.

"The date thing?" The woman sighed at Jaiden's response.

"He wanted to go out with that girl, and you said no and that he needs to stay home studying all weekend? Remember? The huge fight you and he got in?"

Jaiden's stomach sank. He had always sworn to himself that he would be a different kind of parent. More understanding. More chill. And now, here he was, almost exactly like his dad.

"I changed my mind," he told the woman on the phone. *I'm going to be different.* "Let him go out. He's a kid. He deserves to act like one."

LAURA WIPED the tears from her eyes. She had walked into an apartment and saw a man putting clothes into a suitcase. Somehow she knew this guy was her husband. *I'm married,* she had thought excitedly.

She barely got the word hello out before he started yelling, and without realizing it, she was yelling back. She didn't even know what they were fighting about but the words coming out of her mouth were out of her control. She felt like she was right and he was wrong, and he should apologize, but he didn't. He wanted her to apologize. She started crying. He started crying. And then he slammed the door behind him when he left.

She had always said to herself that she would be a better wife than her mom had been. That she would do better. That she would do whatever it took to stay together with whoever she ended up marrying. The sound of the door slamming echoed in her head. She choked back a sob and thought, *maybe it's more complicated than I thought.*

ELIJAH RAN out of the store he had walked into and back into the main part of the mall. He put his hands on his knees and tried to catch his breath. He never should've walked through that door. He hated what he was feeling right now. Grief and guilt.

"Eli?" He looked up and saw Stella sitting with her back against a wall. She had her knees tucked into her chest, and it looked like she had been crying. He walked over and slid down to sit next to her. "What did you see?"

He didn't want to tell her. He didn't want to talk about it. He opened his mouth, but no words would come out.

"I, uh." She hiccuped and then took a deep breath, deciding to tell her experience. "I walked into this house, and I was a mom with kids and stuff then someone knocks on the door, and this old lady is standing there. My first thought was that it was my grandma, cause she looked like her. But then I realized it was my mom." Stella wiped her cheeks. The tears wouldn't stop, though. "She walked in and was talking to everyone, and I, of course, was freaked out cause my mom isn't like in my life or anything. She comes and goes.

"So I go to my phone and try to find my grandma's number but I can't. I ask my mom, and she tells me I haven't seen my grandma since I was a kid. No grandma, cousins, none of the family." Stella looked at Elijah. "I always used to think life would be better if my mom had raised me cause that's what moms are supposed to do, but this whole thing just showed that I wouldn't have my grandma like I have her now. It's so confusing." She put her head in her hands.

"My mom and I don't talk about my dad since he died." Stella raised her head when Elijah started speaking. "It makes me so mad. And I would say to myself that if I was in her shoes, I would handle it all the right way. So, in there, I was married and had a kid and my wife died." Stella gasped. "Now, I'm not so sure there's a perfect right way to handle it when bad stuff happens."

"Dang," she whispered.

"Maybe you didn't have your mom," Elijah told her. "But at least you have someone. Grandmas are moms too."

Stella nodded and sniffled. "Thanks."

A door slamming made them look up and see Adam coming down the hallway. His face was twisted in anger. His stomping ceased when he saw Elijah and Stella. He walked slowly over to them, his hands stuffed in his pockets. "Hey," he mumbled.

"Hey," they responded in unison.

"Did it suck for you guys, too?" he asked.

They nodded.

"Apparently I'm a jerk," Adam said. That caught Elijah off guard.

"I could've told you that," Stella smiled.

Adam chuckled, "I was this business guy with my own office and everything and I thought it was cool, but, uh. No one liked me. I overheard them saying it. Calling me names and stuff."

"Sorry," Elijah said.

"Do you guys feel that?" Stella asked. Adam looked around and Elijah nodded. The mall was trembling, just slightly but enough to be concerning.

"Let's find the others," Adam said.

Elijah helped Stella up, and they tried to keep their balance, but the shaking was getting worse.

"Does Cirque have earthquakes?" Elijah asked.

"Let's hope so," Stella said. "Cause if not." She didn't have to finish her sentence for the boys to know where she was going. *The Shadows.*

"Hey!" Jaiden yelled. He and Laura were running towards them. "Let's get out of here!"

"How?" Adam asked.

"Way we came?" Jaiden wasn't so sure it was going to be that easy.

They could hear crashing and glass breaking. The commotion sounded like it was coming from behind them. And it was getting closer.

"You guys look normal!" Stella yelled. Suddenly, everyone looked like a kid again. "Does that mean there's something wrong with wherever we are?"

"Probably," Laura shouted.

"I don't see the door!" Adam looked around frantically.

The kids screamed and ducked when store windows began to shatter all around them. Glass rained and they flinched at the harsh sounds of the destruction. It was like someone was running along smashing store after store after store. Everyone covered their ears and kept low to the ground during the explosions.

How are we going to get out of here? Jaiden worried. A blinding light caused every pair of eyes to squint.

"Are you hurt?" Elijah looked up to see R.L. They were back in the Hall of Choice.

"I'm good," Laura said.

R.L. looked over everyone and breathed a sigh of relief. "We have a problem," he said.

"Were we not supposed to go in there? I'm–"

The ringleader cut off Elijah's apology, "You're welcome anywhere. No need to be sorry. The problem is the Shadows, I'm afraid." The ringleader dreaded giving them this news.

"What happened?" Jaiden asked at the same time Stella asked, "What did they do?"

"They've gotten a hold of my keys,' R.L. said. Laura remembered the huge keyring R.L. had shown them. "They're in there right now." The group followed R.L.'s gaze to the Door of Desire. "We've gotten a couple of the doors secure, but we're too late for this one, that one" –he pointed to the Door of Opportunity– "and the Lost Room."

"What do we do?" Adam demanded.

The ringleader's fiery eyes burned bright, "We take back our circus."

PART THREE

19. A PLAN

"All I'm saying is R.L. was mad dramatic with the whole, 'we take back our circus' thing," Stella imitated the ringleader's low voice. "And now we're just training like everything is fine."

Jaiden shrugged his shoulders. "I don't know. He said we'd talk about it today. Besides, what are we even supposed to do?" He and Stella sat on the bleachers in the circus ring, taking a break from their training.

Stella's knee bounced up and down nervously. She and Julie had worked on getting her more comfortable with riding Nova at different speeds all morning, and it was almost time to start practicing acrobatic tricks. Stella wanted to throw up with nerves.

"What's wrong with you?" Jaiden asked her. He stretched out his arms in front of him. His muscles were aching.

"Julie wants me to stand on top of my horse while she runs like a hundred miles an hour."

"Big deal," Jaiden said, earning a scoff and punch in the

arm. "I have to get shot out of a canon, a legit canon, and land in a net—hopefully."

"Horses can kill you. She could throw me off. I could fall and break my arms and legs," Stella argued loudly. And then in a lower voice she said, "But, I guess the canon is scary too."

"You think?" Jaiden groaned as Arlo called him over.

"Good luck," Stella laughed.

ELIJAH LAUGHED as he did flip after flip on the trampoline. Adam listened closely as Hank helped him prepare to do a flip without the trampoline. Adam positioned his body and took a deep breath.

"Jump," Hank instructed.

Adam could barely believe it when he landed on his feet. He almost lost his balance, but he adjusted himself and was able to stay standing. He panted and looked up at Hank, who was grinning from ear to ear.

"Good job!" Elijah called.

"Thanks," Adam replied.

Elijah couldn't help the shocked look on his face at Adam's friendly voice. He had been a lot nicer lately but Elijah was still surprised every time. *Who would've thought we would be like this,* he mused. *Who would've thought we'd be joining a circus?* He chuckled under his breath.

LAURA WATCHED as Amos and his mom interacted. Etta said something that made him laugh, and she patted his cheek lovingly. They continued their banter back and forth, making their mother-son relationship seem so effortless.

I wish I was like that with my parents. Laura couldn't remember the last time she laughed and joked with her mom. She was more that way with her dad, but now she was just angry with him about his girlfriend. *He didn't even want to be with me.* Her stomach twisted up, and she felt her eyes prick with emotion.

"Hey." Etta joined her on the couch.

Laura just forced a smile out.

"Whatcha thinking about?" Etta's soothing voice made Laura want to spill her heart and soul out to her.

"Nothing." But of course, she chickened out.

"Are you missing home? Missing your parents?" Etta rested her elbow on the top of the couch and leaned her head against her hand.

"Not really. Besides, I doubt they miss me." *Maybe just my mom, but she's probably relieved not to have to deal with my dad or me.*

"I'm sure that's not true," Etta said. Laura didn't respond. "Being a parent is just as hard as being a kid."

Laura remembered what she had walked into when they went through the Door of Desire. Etta had a point, only a few minutes of marriage, and Laura knew it was harder than she ever realized.

"Parents are just kids with a few more years on them," Etta quipped. "We're all just trying to figure life out until we're out of life."

Laura pondered that. She responded quietly, "I guess." She realized she was absent-mindedly rubbing the mark on her arm. "Amos said that we're all marked our specific act for a reason."

"That's true," Etta confirmed.

"What's yours? Why do you think you were marked as a

clown?" Laura had been trying to figure out what her reason was for days but kept coming up empty.

Etta traced her own mark as she spoke, "I needed to find joy again. I was sad, very sad for most of my life. Being marked as a clown taught me to laugh again." Etta looked up at Laura. "This family in Cirque, in Clown Alley, showed me how to have fun, how to still be able to smile even when things hurt." Etta's smile lit up her eyes.

"Wow." Laura couldn't help but smile. "I don't know what my reason is."

"You will," Etta assured her. "You will."

DINNER HAD ENDED, and Barnaby announced to the dining hall that R.L. requested everyone to meet in the Commons. The chatter died down when the ringleader came out of the door at the top of the stairs that led to the Hall of Choice. He overlooked his circus with concern.

"As you know, the shadows have infiltrated our home. They now have taken over three of the rooms in the Hall of Choice. They are tearing them apart piece by piece." R.L.'s hands clenched around the banister in front of him.

The crowd murmured and whispered to each other. The new recruits all shared worried looks.

"The shadows' goal is to destroy Cirque and then Ekklesia. They wish to see us fall. They have gone too far this time." R.L.'s chest heaved, but he did his best to keep his composure.

"Oh my," a woman whispered. Elijah turned to see Amelia standing next to him. Her eyes were watering with tears.

"There is only one way that the shadows could have gotten through the doors." R.L. paused.

Everyone was holding their breath. Half of Cirque knew exactly what the ringleader's next words would be, but didn't want to believe it to be true. The other half felt anxiety rise at not knowing what was going on.

"Someone in this circus gave the shadows' my keys," R.L.'s voice was a whisper. Saying those words seemed to physically pain him.

The room erupted with anger, sobs, and some shouts of accusation.

"Enough," R.L. boomed.

He is pissed, Adam thought. He didn't think the ringleader could get this angry.

R.L. sighed, "Two of our family members have gotten wrapped up in the shadows' scheme. They handed over the keys and are now with the shadows through their door, which is unlocked now."

"Do you know who?" Laura whispered to Amos. He stood with her and the others. He shook his head, his eyebrows creased in worry.

"We were able to secure the rest of Cirque, but we are weakened right now. We must put the rooms back in order, rescue our family from the shadows, and lock the Dark Door once again," R.L. declared.

"They betrayed us!" a Side Show performer yelled.

"Yes," the ringleader choked out. He wiped the tears from his eyes. "But we will not betray them," R.L.'s concern morphed into determination. "We will bring them home. Cirque is a place of second chances, chances that everyone has needed. If we stop reaching out a hand to those who need it, then we become shadows ourselves." R.L. closed his eyes for a minute. When he opened them, he smiled and straightened his shoulders.

"We have work to do. If you will all report to your trainers, they will give you instructions. My new recruits." The group looked to R.L. "You can join me up here."

The kids walked up the stairs, and R.L. held the door open so they could enter the Hall of Choice. The tension was thick in the hallway. The once beautiful gold Door of Desire was now covered in something like black ink. It was oozing from inside the room. The Door of Opportunity was cracked so bad you couldn't see anything in the glass. And the once beautiful wooden Door to the Lost Room was rotting more and more each minute. There was no sound of music coming from the other side, only a draft of ice-cold air.

"Who did it?" Adam asked. "Who took the keys?"

"Two performers, a fire breather and a creator," R.L. answered.

"Creator?" Stella asked.

"Costumes, sets, things like that," Barnaby told her.

"I called you here with me because I need your help," R.L. spoke with urgency and desperation. "Tomorrow, I will be going through the Dark Door to get back our circus freaks and my keys."

Jaiden glanced at the Dark Door and shivered. He did not want to see where the shadows lived.

"And us?" Elijah asked.

"You will be separating, and with some help from a few of your trainers, you will bring order back to the rooms we have already lost." The group shared surprised looks with one another. "Each room is fueled by light, the exact opposite of shadows. The only way they can continue to exist in there is if they keep the light out. You have to turn it on again." R.L. looked to each recruit.

"Is it like a light switch? A lamp?" Stella asked.

"It's different for each room. A fireplace in the Lost Room, a light switch in the room of Desire, and a mirrorball in the room of Opportunity."

"Mirrorball?" Jaiden questioned.

"More commonly known as a disco ball," Barnaby clarified.

"All you have to do is bring light back in, and the shadows are gone," R.L.'s eyes glazed over for a second as he stared at the Door of Shadows.

"I have a feeling it's not gonna be as easy as it sounds," said Laura.

R.L. chuckled and nodded his head. "You would be right. But, I know this"–the ringleader took a step closer to his recruits– "if anyone is going to be able to do it, it's all of you."

"How? I mean," Adam spoke emphatically with his hands. "You really think *we* can do this?"

The rest of the group was quiet, all thinking the same thing and all wanting to hear what their ringleader would have to say. R.L. and Barnaby shared a look, both remembering how Barnaby asked the same question not too long ago.

R.L. took a step forward. His face settled into a mischievous expression, "You have been recruits. You have been trainees. You have been normal, so to speak, and you have been thrown into the world of Cirque. You have been scared. You have been brave. You have been strangers. You have become family. Now, it's time to be shadow chasers."

Laura gasped. She could've sworn she saw a flash of lightning in R.L.'s eyes.

"It may be hard to believe," R.L. continued, "but the shadows are scared of 2 things. Me" –he put his hand on his chest– "and all of you." He pointed a finger at each kid in front of him.

"For real?" Stella stared in disbelief.

"For real." R.L. stepped forward again as if to emphasize how crucial it was for them to believe it. "You scare them because you are stronger than them. If you trust me and follow my instructions, you'll bring the light back into those rooms and chase them out. They'll go back to where they came from."

"Shadow chasers," Adam tested out the title on his tongue.

20. A LIGHT SWITCH

"What do you think is gonna happen today?" Elijah gulped.

The kids sat on hardcover vintage suitcases that were stacked near the train. Instead of the exciting rumble the mornings in the Side Show usually had, everyone was deep in thought. They spoke in hushed voices and comforted each other about the day to come.

"I think we're gonna kick some shadow butt," Stella meant to sound more confident than what her voice portrayed. She was freaking out like everyone else.

"Last time we saw the shadows," Laura sighed. "It sucked. Majorly sucked."

"But R.L. said we can fight them. We're gonna be fine," Jaiden assured his friends. "We're gonna do what we gotta do in those rooms and be back at that weird table for dinner."

They all laughed at his comment and felt a little more confident. They saw Barnaby approaching where they sat, and they knew it was time.

.   .   .

"THE GENERAL and his team are going to make sure everything is good here while we're gone. Barnaby will stay right here in the Hall until we all get back," R.L. ran through the details of the plan.

He had introduced the group to the General earlier. He was a tall muscular man with a dark mustache. He wore a very serious expression and rarely spoke unless he was asked a direct question. Even though he was intimidating, he also made everyone feel secure. It was obvious how committed he was to keeping everyone safe.

Elijah waved at Evan, the knife thrower. He was standing next to an older woman who had her white hair pulled up in a tight bun. She wore a black long sleeve shirt, black jeans, and thick black boots.

"That's Annette," Hank whispered to Eli. "She's the trainer for the fire breathers."

Elijah nodded. He observed his fellow recruits and the others joining them; Julie, Hank, Arlo, and Logan.

"You know your teams." R.L. smiled warmly at everyone who stood with him in the Hall of Choice. "Be safe and be brave. The shadows can only hurt you as much as you let them. Do everything in your power to block out their voices. Don't look at what they try to show you. Make your voice, and your team's voice louder than theirs."

R.L. stood in front of the Door of Shadows with Annette and Evan by his side, "And so we begin."

THE DOOR of Desire closed behind Jaiden, Arlo, and Logan. The room looked nothing like it had when Jaiden and the others were there before. Instead of a mall, there were just four empty white walls.

"This isn't what it looked like before," Jaiden whispered. Even his whisper echoed loudly in the room.

"The room forms into different things depending on who goes into it. It shows you what you desire and usually shows the truth behind it, or morphs it to show you that what you desire isn't what you need," Arlo explained in a hushed tone.

"Where are we supposed to find a light switch?" Logan wondered. As far as he could see there was nothing, just white. Even the floors were white.

"I guess we walk until we see it," Arlo said.

"It's gotta be on one of the walls," Jaiden figured.

They started walking forward towards the wall in front of them. Jaiden reached out his hand, thinking they had reached it, but he grasped at nothing. He took several more steps forward and reached out again but he was no closer to the wall.

"Guys?" Jaiden gulped.

Arlo walked to the right and Logan to the left. Jaiden kept going forward. No matter how far he went, he never neared a wall. He turned around to yell for the others, but they were still close together, like they hadn't walked anywhere at all.

They shared looks of worry and then Logan made it worse, "The door we came through is gone."

"What?" Arlo panicked.

A loud bang made them flinch. They couldn't tell where it was coming from. It sounded like the same one that hit the train cars on Jaiden's first night at Cirque. They felt like they were being watched, goosebumps raised on their skin.

"I think somethings coming," Logan trembled.

The banging started again louder than before and one after another, no pause in between.

"Run!" Arlo shouted.

They took off. The walls just expanded in front of them as they went. Jaiden didn't know what was worse. Something chasing them or the fact that they were running at full speed and getting absolutely nowhere.

Jaiden fell backwards when an ear-splitting screech came from right in front of him. Logan and Arlo stumbled to a stop beside him. Everything was quiet now. No bangs, no screeches. Just the sound of three boys out of breath.

All around them, everywhere they looked, was nothing. Jaiden tried to calm his breathing down as he stood up. *Freaking out is not gonna help us or Cirque,* he told himself.

"Okay," Arlo motioned for Jaiden and Logan to come close and he whispered. "We know there's a light switch somewhere in here that the shadows don't want us to find."

"And they have control of the room right now," Logan added.

"So they can make us see what they want us to see?" Arlo nodded yes to Jaiden's question.

"Maybe this isn't real," Logan looked around.

"R.L. always says that Cirque is ours just like it is his," Arlo's voice changed from scared to excited, "so if he would know where the switch is—"

"Then the shadows are assuming we do too," Jaiden interrupted. "So maybe we do." *There's no way. That's too risky,* Jaiden tried to shake the negative voice from his mind.

"One way to find out," Arlo offered. Logan and Jaiden nodded in agreement.

"This way," Jaiden said before he could overthink it. He was going to trust his instincts. He was gonna take the risk.

He walked left, and at first, the wall stayed the same. Plain, white, and just moving farther away. *Don't look at what they try to show you,* R.L.'s voice rang in his head. Jaiden stopped walking, Arlo and Logan following his actions. He closed his eyes, counted to three, and then opened them again.

When he opened them the room had changed drastically. The walls were navy blue instead of white and decorated with empty picture frames. An antique rug took up most of the floor space with a couch and armchair sitting atop it.

"Are you seeing this?" Jaiden asked, not taking his eyes away from the sight in front of him.

"Yeah," Arlo and Logan answered in unison.

"I think that's it." Jaiden pointed in front of them.

Between two tall empty bookcases was a few inches of wall and a light switch with a white cover around it. All they had to do was walk across the room and flip it.

"Seems too easy," Logan muttered.

"Definitely," Arlo agreed. "But let's go."

As soon as they took their first steps towards the switch, the screeching and banging started up again, somehow louder than before. They covered their ears and stopped walking as soon as the horrible sounds assaulted them. Like a glitch, the room was switching from the furniture-filled one to the empty white walls. Logan howled out, sounding more like a dog than ever in his life. His head was aching from the noise.

"Jaiden! You're closest!" Arlo yelled.

Jaiden kept his hands over his ears and stood back up. He began to run, but something grabbed at his ankle, causing him to trip. He looked down at his leg that was trapped in a trim shadowy grip.

As he looked at the black mist that held him, he could just barely make out the voices of his parents. Their words sounded familiar. He stared harder, wanting to know what they were saying.

He was pulled out of the trance when Arlo hooked his arms under Jaiden's armpits and dragged him away. Logan ran towards the boys, going right through the shadows, making them disperse.

Arlo pushed Jaiden away and towards the wall with the switch. He and Logan stood ready to attempt to fight the dark figures that were headed straight for them. Arlo's head pounded, and Logan wanted nothing more than to close his eyes and hide. But they stood, covering Jaiden, hoping he could get to the switch.

As soon as Jaiden flipped the switch, the shadows exploded into tiny pieces, flying away like bats who were scared out of their cave. The screeching and banging faded away as the room cleared until the only ones standing were the human cannonballs and the dog-faced boy.

21. A CIRCUS TENT

R.L. walked with purpose. Annette and Evan trailed close behind. Their feet stomped in puddles that pooled in the broken concrete. They were headed to the shadows' circus tent, a backward attempt to be like Cirque Des Èlus. But to get to the tent, they had to get through the city. Annette always thought the shadows' city looked like Ekklesia if Ekklesia had been burned and ravaged. She had been here once before and never intended on returning.

Garbage littered every inch of the ground. Rats scurried one after another like they were playing a game of tag. Dry lightning flashed across the sky, illuminating the desolate streets. Evan shivered from the cold air. The buildings they passed looked abandoned, but every once in a while, they'd pass a house or apartment with a light on.

R.L. knew they were being followed. He felt it the second they entered through the threshold. Shadows were lurking behind them and up ahead of them. Dark eyes watched their every move. With a wave of his hand, R.L. could get rid of them, but there were bigger things to focus on right now. Besides, he loved putting on a good show.

They approached a puddle-filled blacktop with a circus tent crookedly standing in the middle of it, the top of it leaning too much to the right. Black and white stripes loomed against the black sky with white crackling across it every few minutes.

The ringleader reached forward to pull the curtain to the entrance open, but a rushing sound coming from behind stopped him. He turned around and looked back where they had come from. Annette and Evan followed his gaze. Dozens of shadows were headed straight at them, moving fast like they were running from something.

R.L. stepped to the side and held the curtain open. The shadows flew like bats wildly into the tent. R.L. Laughed and looked at his fire breather and knife thrower.

"Looks like the recruits are succeeding," Annette said, impressed.

The ringleader nodded, "One door down, two to go."

22. A DISCO BALL

"**D**ang," Stella awed as they entered through the Door of Opportunity.

Glass covered the floor. Rows of mirrors went on for as far as they could see, but every single one was shattered. It was almost completely dark, a single light on a wall flickering on and off. Stella, Julie, and Elijah gripped flashlights in their hands.

"What does this room do?" Elijah asked Julie.

She took a moment to answer. Her heart broke as she looked at the mess before her. "These mirrors, they show you what could be, opportunity. Things you could do, could be, could have."

Stella looked down into pieces of glass surrounding her feet. She looked different in every single shard. The pieces were small. She could just make out that she was wearing glasses in one and what looked like some kind of uniform in several others.

"That's cool," Elijah winced at the crunch of glass under

his feet. He felt guilty, but there was no way to avoid it. Fragments of opportunity were everywhere they stepped.

They continued walking slowly, mostly because no one could stand the sound of glass constantly breaking under them. Stella pointed her flashlight all around, trying to find the disco ball, which she thought was hilarious.

"I can't believe we're looking for a disco ball right now. A disco ball is gonna save the circus," she announced dramatically.

"Tone it down there, drama queen," Julie retorted.

Stella just scoffed and kept moving her flashlight erratically.

"We're in a room of mirrors," Elijah reasoned. "Makes sense we'd be looking for a disco ball or a mirrorball, as R.L. called it. Literally, a ball of mirrors."

"Yeah, I guess," Stella muttered.

The room looked empty except for the mirrors. There didn't seem to be an end to the room either, it would take them forever to find what they were looking for. The shadows watched from corners and in the darkness behind some of the mirrors.

"Do you hear that?" Julie whispered.

The three of them looked to their right. Pieces of glass were rising off of the floor. They began to fill up three mirrors but in a jagged pattern. None of the glass fit together properly. Once the mirrors were mostly filled, the reflection they showed was a distorted image.

In one mirror, Stella saw herself sitting alone in a dark room crying. Elijah recognized the hospital walls and floor in the other mirror, and it was him hooked up to the same machine his father had been. Beeping sounds pierced his ears. And Julie, she saw her younger self hiding behind a couch as two adults screamed at each other. *Mom and dad,* she thought. She felt small and powerless as she watched.

Stella felt her stomach sinking and her chest tightening. She was alone. She's always been alone. She'll always be alone. Her mom left because she didn't want her. Her dad left because he didn't want her. She had no friends. Her grandma wouldn't be around forever. She was alone. All alone.

Elijah's biggest fear was coming true right in front of him. He was dying in a crappy hospital room. *Beep. Beep. Beep.* The noise taunted him. He saw his face changing color with illness. Life draining from his eyes.

"No, no, no," Julie muttered. She shut her eyes tightly and shook her head. *It's not real.* She looked at the kids next to her. They were both crying but she doubted they realized it.

Stella screamed as the glass that had been torturing her was once again shattered and on the ground. Julie held tight to the flashlight she had smashed the mirror with and did the same to the one in front of Elijah. He jolted back and frantically looked around.

"What was that?" Stella shrieked.

"Shadows," Julie growled. "Come on."

She marched forward with new determination, Elijah and Stella feeling it too. They were tired of the shadows messing with their minds. *Don't look next time,* Stella scolded herself. They could hear glass gathering like it had done before. Each mirror they passed tried to show them something painful.

"Don't look," Julie commanded.

"Don't look, don't look, don't look," Elijah whispered to himself. He didn't want to see it again anyway, him in the hospital bed. He shuddered.

"Hey," Stella pointed her flashlight to their right. There was a heavy black smoke hovering over something round.

More shadows came from all directions and thickened the blanket of smoke, obviously trying to guard it.

"That has to be it," Julie said. They walked closer to it.

"They're not very good at hiding things," Stella mumbled. Wherever she would point her flashlight the blackness would thin out a little bit.

"How do we get rid of it?" Eli grimaced at the slithering way the shadows moved.

Julie didn't seem to know the answer, but she leaned forward and touched the mist. Where her hand connected to it, the mist dissolved, and a tiny section of the mirrorball could be seen. Stella and Elijah joined her in quickly wiping away the darkness shrouding the ball. They could see themselves in it eventually. The shadows tried to cover it back up wherever their hands weren't touching it.

A grumbling sound from all around them got increasingly loud. The shadows were getting angry. The glass began two tremble under their feet. Something bad was about to happen.

"Help me lift it." They did as Julie said and followed her as she led them towards the middle of the room. Above them, a wire with a clasp at the end hung from the ceiling.

"How are we supposed to get it up there? I don't remember seeing a ladder or anything? And last I checked, none of our circus acts are flying," Stella ranted.

"Stella, your commentary is very unhelpful," Julie told her.

"This whole situation is very unhelpful," she started up again, but Elijah cut her off.

"I have an idea." He knew he might regret it, but it was the only option that seemed to be available.

Stella looked as the glass slowly rose off the ground, "hurry."

"Julie, you're gonna have to lift me, and I'm gonna stand on your shoulders," Eli spoke as fast as he could. "Stella, you hand the mirrorball up to me."

"You're crazy," Stella exclaimed.

"He's right," Julie said. "I've been around long enough to know a few acrobat tricks. I can do it."

"Alright." Elijah took a deep breath.

Elijah and Julie got in position, and in a swift movement, he was standing on her shoulders. He knew she wouldn't be able to hold him for long. He had to act fast. Keeping his balance, he reached forward and grabbed the ball from a struggling Stella.

Every shard raised from the floor and pointed their direction. "Hurry up, Eli!" she urged. In a second, the pieces formed one giant cracked mirror around them. Stella looked up at Eli who focused on the disco ball. Julie closed her eyes. They all fought to ignore the scenes the mirrors were playing out.

Hospitals and loneliness and screaming parents.

Dying and despair and hiding.

Fear and crying and running.

Elijah silently thanked Hank for making them work out in training sessions, and he marveled at how he was even able to lift the mirrorball. *'You were meant for this,'* R.L.'s voice echoed in his mind.

Julie swayed slightly under his weight.

He grunted as he lifted the ball and hooked it.

He flinched at the powerful light it released and went tumbling right off Julie's shoulders. His eyes opened in shock after he realized he had landed on his feet.

A blinding glow filled the room. The jagged wall around them dispersed. The pieces flew to their proper mirrors. They settled in, all becoming smooth, unbroken surfaces showcasing possibility once again.

Stella covered her ears from the shrieks the shadows released as they tried to escape. Dark figures fluttered above their heads, all trying to be the first one out. The door of Opportunity flung open and every last creature was gone.

Stella panted, "I guess a disco ball really did save the circus."

23. A FIREPLACE

"Go! Go! Go!" Hank shouted at Adam and Laura.

The three of them took off running, trying to avoid the flames coming after them. Everything in The Lost Room was on fire. As soon as they had walked through the door the flames were on either side of them, and growing larger by the second. It wasn't a normal fire though. It was gray and cold. *A shadow fire,* Laura thought.

Even though it didn't look or feel like regular fire, it was still turning to ashes all the hopes and dreams that were stored in the cluttered, castle-like room. The menagerie of chandeliers that hung from the ceiling trembled from the shadows' booming laughter and cackling. Smoke made it hard to see where they were running.

"We have to find the fireplace," Laura hissed when her hip ran into something hard.

"Everything's on fire. It's bright in here. I thought the shadows were taking all the light," Adam questioned.

"False light!" Hank yelled. "Here!" He turned and ducked

under a table, pulling the kids with him. The three of them huddled together, using the table as a momentary hiding spot.

Smoke hung around them. Streams of black passed by them every few seconds. Burnt paper fell like snow off the table above them. A painting of a beautiful scenic beach next to them shriveled up.

"False light?" Laura whispered.

Hank nodded. "Shadows are copycats. Look" –Lily and Adam followed Hank's line of sight– "the fireplace is over there."

Dark gray stones shaped a fireplace large enough to fit three Hanks standing straight up with his arms stretched out. Its mantle held books and candle holders. A thick gold frame hung above it, but the fire had burnt away whatever picture had been inside of it.

"Plan?" Adam turned to Hank with a brow raised.

"Plan," Hank repeated, his eyes set on the cold, empty fireplace.

"Distraction," Laura suggested. "One of us distracts while the others get the fire going?"

They jumped at the sound of something heavy falling from across the room. If the word slimy had a sound, it would describe the shadows' laughter.

"You start the fire," Hank said to the recruits. He took out a small book of matches from his pocket and put it in Adam's hand.

"I don't know," Adam's voice wavered. *This is too much pressure,* he thought. His mother's voice momentarily invaded his thoughts. *You can't do anything right!*

"Wait–" Laura's attempt at convincing Hank of a different plan was cut off.

"You got this," Hank reassured them. "Now."

Hank crawled out from the table and sprinted towards the way they came. A split second later a group of shadows were chasing him. Adam looked worriedly at Laura.

"We got this," she said. Her wavering voice betrayed her. She tried again. "We got this."

Adam nodded at her attempts to sound confident.

She took a deep breath and then took his hand. They bolted to the fireplace. The smoke had thickened making it more difficult to see. *Just run straight,* Laura yelled in her mind.

She shrieked as a gray flame touched her. She heard her mother crying in the bathroom and realized she was sitting in the hallway of her house. *How did I get here? What's going on?*

"Laura!" Adam yelled for the third time. Finally she blinked her eyes and recognized him. "What just happened?"

"Don't let the fire touch you. It took me to like, a memory or something. A bad memory." She pushed his arm out of the way of a flame that bursted up from a pile of books.

"Come on!" He ran in front of her and pulled her along the rest of the way.

They could hear Hank yelling at the shadows, trying to keep their attention. For the most part they focused on him but Adam could see wisps of black coming their way.

"I don't think there's enough logs." Laura pointed to the small bundle stacked in the middle.

They looked around and saw a pile of wood off to the side. Laura rushed over to start collecting some. Adam attempted to strike a match, but only a few sparks were appearing, nothing more. His hands were getting slick with sweat as his nerves skyrocketed.

"Come on!" Adam barked in frustration.

"Adam," Laura pleaded. She tossed her armload of logs into the fireplace and then went back for another one.

The screech of a shadow hit Adam's ears before the shadow itself flung into his face. His body fell backward, his hand landing on top of a burning guitar.

"All you do is cost me money. You need to get a job to help out around here," Adam's mom yelled.

He shook his head. *No, this isn't real.*

"I buy you things and you don't even take care of them."

"This isn't real!" He screamed.

He gasped as Laura appeared in front of him. She emptied her arms and then helped him up. Her expression asked if he was okay, he nodded and got out another match.

Shadows were charging at them from the other side of the room, black globs moving faster than Laura would've liked.

"Adam!" She screamed.

"Got it!" The match finally lit, and he tossed it onto the logs.

The shadows kept moving forward and nothing in the room changed. Laura looked at the fireplace to see the fire had died out. Adam lit another match but the fire wouldn't catch. Laura bent down to help him but she had no luck either. They both screamed when a figure appeared between them.

"Hank!" Laura yelled relieved.

"It won't light," Adam told him.

Hank leaned into the fireplace and rearranged the logs. Putting the smaller ones on top and moving the larger ones around. Laura faced the room and gasped at the shadows closing in on them.

"You scare them because you are stronger than them," R.L.'S voice filled Laura's head.

She stood up and took a step away from the boys. She ignored Adam's protest. The shadows were getting closer and closer. She faintly heard Hank tell Adam to try again. Laura took a deep breath and stood with her shoulders back and her head held high. The sound of the creatures rushing toward her didn't make her back down like they had hoped. She wasn't afraid.

Every shadow heading toward her stopped in their tracks. They were frozen. Hank and Adam were focused on lighting the fire and Laura stood with no fear. There was no one for the shadows to mess with. Laura smiled.

Adam pushed Laura to the ground. Ceiling-high flames erupted from behind them. The fire had caught and now blazed fiercely. Laura looked to her right to see Hank on the ground too. He was watching the shadows.

Their forms twisted and terrible screeching filled the room. They recoiled and flew quickly to the door taking the thick smoke with them. A soft crackling brought comfort as the flames of the fireplaces lowered and settled into a cozy blaze.

"Are you okay?" Hank stood and helped the kids up.

"Yeah," Adam grunted.

Laura nodded and dusted herself off. Ashes covered their clothes and faces. The three of them looked around at the destruction. Paper scattered everywhere, paint splattered on the walls and floor. But, the chandeliers were lit and the sconces on the walls were illuminated. The Lost Room was restored.

"I knew it wouldn't be as easy as R.L. Made it seem," Laura joked.

Hank and Adam gave her exasperated looks. And then, Adam laughed. He laughed a laugh of relief, adrenaline, and accomplishment. *We did it.*

Hank joined in and Laura too. To anyone else, they would've looked completely crazy. Three people covered in ash, dust, and sweat. Cracking up in a room of random half-burnt items. If you were to ask R.L. he would smile and say that they were definitely crazy. In the best possible way.

24. A SHADOW

R.L., Annette, and Evan walked confidently into the black and white circus tent. It took a minute for their eyes to adjust to the lack of light. Shadows hovered above the bleachers as if they were sitting in them. Distorted music played from the band and a single shadow sat above them all, Dominus. The shadows thought of him as their king. R.L. had other names he preferred to call him.

"My recruits are ridding Cirque of your shadows as we speak," R.L.'s voice held authority. He knew he had the upper hand.

Dominus leaned forward as the ringleader and his circus freaks walked towards him. "We'll see if they fully succeed," he hissed. "Either way, I have brought trouble to your paradise. I have succeeded in proving that even the ringleader's circus trembles." He raised his arms and spoke as if he were announcing a great accomplishment to his shadows. Guttural howls came from them. Evan shivered at the sound.

"You have only succeeded in reminding us of your vile ways," Annette fumed.

Dominus chuckled. "I remember you."

Annette clenched her jaw.

"You came here once, long ago," he taunted. "You abandoned the very circus you stand here today representing. And *I* am vile? Ha!"

"Enough," R.L. Demanded. "I am here for my people."

"They betrayed you," Dominus said in a "duh" tone.

"Betrayed you!" echoed his followers.

"I have come. For. My. People," R.L. ground out the words and took a step forward as he spoke each one.

The Shadow King stood and was about to speak before more of his followers burst through the opening of the tent, squealing all the way. Not a second after they entered, another group scurried in. The howls of defeat brought a smile to the ringleader's face.

"I think that's all the doors," Evan said with a laugh.

"I believe you're right," R.L. stepped forward. Dominus faltered for a second before trying to cover it up with a growl. R.L. left no room for discussion in his voice, "now, give me what is mine, and we will be gone."

"Ahhhh!" Dominus let out a deranged howl and hurled himself right at the ringleader.

Every shadow in the tent followed his lead and charged at Annette and Evan with ridiculous speed. Annette pulled out a torch and lighter from inside her jacket. She plunged the fire right into the shadows, causing them to screech and cower away. Evan held a knife in each hand, powerful knives forged by R.L. himself. They were created with light, a light that no shadow could stand. He swiped at the darkness, smiling at their hisses of pain.

R.L. stood calm and collected as the Shadow King wrapped him in his cocoon of inky darkness. Dominus knew R.L. would succeed in what he came there to do, but admitting defeat was not an option. Dominus was too out of his mind to care that he was fighting a losing battle.

"We're done here." R.L. smiled and with one snap of his fingers, Dominus erupted into red glittery dust.

Every shadow in the room stopped what they were doing and before they could make a run for it, they were expelled in the same way. Annette and Evan let out haggard breaths while the red dust fell slowly around them. *Like red snow,* Annette thought.

"Good job," the ringleader told his freaks. "Now, let's get our family."

THE DOOR of Shadows slammed shut behind the group that now stood in the Hall of Choice. Evan turned and locked every bolt on the door before giving the key ring back to his ringleader. Light sobs came from Lauren, the creator. The fire breather, Thomas, stood with his head hung, tears dripped off of his nose onto the floor.

R.L. opened his mouth to speak, but Lauren beat him to it. "I'm so sorry," she cried. "I'm so sorry." Her body shook with her sobs.

R.L. wrapped her in a hug. "I know. You are forgiven." His words and embrace just made her cry harder.

The ringleader looked at Thomas, "And you, Thomas. You're forgiven."

Thomas couldn't even make eye contact with R.L. The guilt and embarrassment made him want to run and hide. He didn't deserve to be here. He didn't deserve to be a part of

Cirque again, not after what he did to them. He had put everyone in danger. He didn't deserve a mark–

"Hey," Annette nudged his arm and brought him out of his thoughts.

Thomas looked at his instructor ashamed.

"I made the mistake too," she said. He looked at her in confusion. "I let the shadows get in my head once, just like you. You're not the first, I wasn't the first, and you won't be the last" –she grabbed his hand and squeezed reassuringly– "what's done is done. What matters now is how you carry on." Annette squeezed Thomas' shoulder comfortingly. "And you will carry on here at Cirque."

Thomas looked to the ringleader.

He nodded his head, agreeing with Annette.

Lauren stepped back from R.L. and wiped her eyes.

"I'm starving," Evan interjected, earning chuckles.

"We're due for a celebration." R.L. hugged Thomas before leading them to the Commons.

All of Cirque was gathered in the Commons once again, waiting to see what had become of their ringleader and those he had set out to rescue. Worry ate up the inside of Lauren and Thomas. They didn't know what to expect from the circus they had hurt.

R.L. leaned forward against the banister of the stairs and addressed the crowd, "Our family is home. The shadows are locked away." His smile was filled with confidence and comfort.

The room burst into cheers, happy sobs, and music. He wouldn't have expected any less. As he walked down the stairs, the sight of Thomas and Lauren being embraced and loved on warmed his heart. Family never gives up on family.

He continued through the room talking to those who

stopped him and hugging those who looked like they needed it. Finally, he found the group he was looking for.

Stella had said something sarcastic that made everyone laugh. Laura sipped from a mug of hot chocolate. Adam stuffed his face with desserts that were being served. Elijah laughed and shook his head at Jaiden as he playfully argued with Stella.

"R.L.!" Laura exclaimed. The group turned their heads to the ringleader.

"Scoot over," Elijah told Jaiden. The boys moved over so R.L. could join them on the couch.

"There aren't enough words to describe how thankful I am to each of you and how proud." R.L. felt tears well up in his eyes. "You have come so far in your time with us."

"It was crazy," Stella told him, waving her hands excitedly as she spoke. "Elijah did a whole acrobat trick to get the disco ball–mirrorball, whatever–hanging again."

"We were in a room on fire, a cold gray fire, and…" Adam recounted their adventure with enthusiasm.

He's happy. The ringleader smiled at the joy that lit up Adam's face.

"The Desire room was creepy," Jaiden joined in.

The group continued to banter about who had it the worse. R.L. just watched, marveling at how much they had grown into their own. His heart sank in his chest at the knowledge that it was almost time for them to go.

"R.L.," Laura addressed the ringleader. "Will the shadows get out again?"

The group was silent as they waited for an answer. They all felt apprehension at the thought of ever seeing the shadows again.

R.L. sighed, "They will always try."

"Why don't you just get rid of them?" Adam asked.

"One day, they'll be gone forever, just not yet. Everything happens in the time it's meant to," R.L. explained. He smiled and stood up to leave. "Enjoy the rest of your night but be ready for training tomorrow. We'll be having a Cirque performance in a few days."

"What?"

"For who?"

"A few days?"

"Performance?"

"Huh?"

R.L. bellowed a laugh at the voices overlapping each other. "We are going to put on a show in celebration of our triumph today. Extra mesmerizing, extra fantastic, and extra special since you will all be in the ring with us."

The kids just gawked at him wide-eyed.

"What?" R.L. chuckled. "You didn't think I had you training for nothing, did you?"

25. A REVELATION

J aiden blinked the sweat out of his eyes as he continued to lift weights. The rest of the circus had been taking it easy for a few days after dealing with the shadows, but Jaiden was pushing himself. He felt ridiculously unprepared for being shot out of a cannon.

"You about ready to give it a go?" Arlo asked Jaiden, stifling a chuckle at the panic that flashed across the trainee's eyes.

"Um, no." Jaiden put his attention back on the weights.

"Jaiden, it's time. Come on," Arlo urged. Jaiden huffed and puffed and complained all the way to the cannon.

He suspiciously eyed the net that he would be landing in. He had jumped into it before from a high platform that the trapeze artists used, but this was going to be entirely different. He was going to be shot high up in the air, almost as high as the top of the tent. He looked at his instructor pleadingly but Arlo wasn't going to change his mind.

"The only way to get over the fear of the cannon," Arlo waited for Jaiden to finish his sentence.

"Is to climb into it," Jaiden's voice was a whisper. He stared at the daunting hunk of metal.

He fastened his helmet on his head. His sweaty palms gripped the ladder tightly as he climbed up to the barrel. *This is crazy. I'm going to get hurt. I can't believe Arlo is making me do this. I can't believe R.L. is letting him.*

"You got this, Jaiden!" Jaiden smiled tightly at Elijah's encouraging voice. It seemed like everyone in the circus ring stopped what they were doing to watch.

Jaiden climbed up and slid feet first down the barrel of the cannon. He took deep breaths but they weren't helping him calm down at all. The barrel was narrow and he knew it was in his head, but it looked like the sides were closing in on him making the space smaller and smaller and smaller.

"Hey." Arlo's head popped up above him.

"Hey." Jaiden gulped in an attempt to get rid of the scratchiness in his throat.

"Do you know why you're the human cannonball?" Jaiden was caught off guard by Arlo's question.

"What? No, I, I have no idea."

"Well," Arlo offered, "maybe because you need to learn to take risks."

"I'm sure there's an easier way to teach that lesson," Jaiden quipped.

Arlo let out a belly laugh and shook his head, "Everything you told me about your parents, about you feeling like you had to secure your future right now, it didn't seem like there was any room there to take chances. To take risks. It seems like there's no room to fly and fail."

Jaiden scrunched his face in thought. Failure was never an option. According to his parents, it was all about making safe and smart choices. "Why would anyone want to fail?" he asked.

"You learn just as much when you hit the ground as when you touch the sky," Arlo replied.

"I get that you're being inspirational, but can we not talk about hitting the ground right now?" Jaiden's exasperated voice made Arlo laugh loudly again.

"Right, right. Point is, you should take risks. You should climb into cannons. You should take chances and be okay with not everything working out. Whatever you decide to do in life, do it cause you love it. Not 'cause you're folding to the pressure of others."

That would be nice, Jaiden thought.

"Alright." Arlo patted the barrel of the cannon. "Let's do this."

"No backing out?" Jaiden whispered.

"That would be doing a disservice to you. Breathe deep, count to thirty, and clench." Arlo's head disappeared and Jaiden tried to breathe as calmly as possible.

1, 2, 3, 4, 5, he could hear distant voices, but his breath and the voice in his head were the loudest things. He got to 20 seconds, and suddenly Arlo's voice rang in his mind, *take risks.*

Jaiden's breath hitched when he heard a clicking of gears. He clenched his body as tight as possible, lifted his head, and put his shoulders back. Then, he was in the air. Blurry red and white stripes were all he saw until he bounced in the net.

He blinked several times to rid the dizziness in his head. The cheers and claps around him sounded so far away. The net trembled as Arlo crawled onto it and towards him.

"How do you feel?" Arlo asked. Jaiden just looked at him dazed. "How do you feel?" he repeated.

"I did it." Jaiden was dumbfounded. He just got shot out of a cannon. He just took the biggest risk of his life.

His body readjusted, and the sounds around him came into focus. Adam and Elijah were shouting something with smiles on their faces. Laura was in some ridiculous clown costume, clapping her life away. And R.L. was there, amid of the cheering crowd of performers, his face beaming with pride.

Then, Jaiden let out the loudest laugh and couldn't stop. "I did it!" he yelled at Arlo before tackling him in a hug.

"Told you!" Arlo chuckled.

Maybe risk-taking is worth it, Jaiden thought to himself. He looked over at the cannon. "Let's go again." He nodded at Arlo's bewildered face. "I want to do it again."

"WHENEVER YOU'RE READY!" Julie shouted.

Stella nodded in response. She leaned forward as Nova galloped round and round the pen. They had been preparing for their first trick, Stella standing up on Nova's back as she ran. She had done pretty well with getting on her knees and then crouching. She hadn't fallen off, which she was taking as a good sign.

She slowly got to her knees. Then she squatted. She kept her eyes focused in front of her. She slowly started to rise, keeping her feet as steady as she could on the saddle. Nova seemed okay. She wasn't getting spooked by Stella standing. Julie watched intently.

Stella smiled wide when she stood up completely as Nova ran. Then, Nova stopped abruptly and sent Stella flying. Julie was there in a second, instructing Nova to run full speed around the pen as a form of correction. She helped Stella off of the ground and they stood in the middle of the round pen as Nova raced around them.

"Ugh!" Stella yelled in frustration.

"You okay?" Julie checked for injuries.

"Yeah, just sore, but I'm okay." Stella rolled her shoulders and her neck a few times.

"Good job, that was incredible." Julie hugged her.

"She threw me off." Stella watched Nova trot in circles. "She's unpredictable."

"She's still learning too," said Julie gently.

"Well, I'm done for the day," Stella's lip trembled. The second in the air and the second hitting the ground had scared her. It was the whole reason she didn't want to do this in the first place.

"Okay, that's fine," Julie made Nova come to a stop.

The three of them stood in the round pen, nobody moving for a moment. Then, Nova walked slowly towards Stella and bowed her head. Stella wanted to pet her, but she was still angry and scared.

"You know," Julie began, "we have to trust even after people hurt us."

"What if all they do is hurt you?" Stella challenged.

"You have to know when to get out of an unhealthy relationship like that, of course. But, you've also got to give second chances. Nova has learned from her mistake, I promise you." Julie nudged her trainee towards the horse.

Stella sighed and cautiously rubbed Nova's forehead.

"Trust is tricky," Julie added.

"For real," Stella grumbled. She smiled at Nova's whinny. They were both learning, as Julie said. "We did good, though, girl. Before you threw me off," she spoke to Nova.

"Horses are like people," Julie laughed. "They can hurt you, but the right ones make life worthwhile."

"That's why I'm an equestrian, huh?" Stella looked at her instructor.

"Is it?" Julie asked,

"'Cause I have to learn to trust again. I have to be able to let people in. Even though I'll get hurt, I can't just shut down." Stella thought about home and how she had no one except her grandma that she trusted because she never gave anyone a chance. She didn't even try to lean on friends because she figured they would all leave too. By isolating herself she figured no one would be able to hurt her. But now she realized she had just been hurting herself.

"I'm very proud of you, Stella," Julie said.

"Thank you" –Stella wrapped her in a hug– "thank you for everything."

"How long do you think we've been here?" Adam asked the group. No one at Cirque ever said what day of the week it was. It felt like they had been there for months now.

"No clue," Jaiden said. He hadn't even thought about it.

"Knowing Cirque, probably way less than we think," Elijah offered.

"Or way more," Adam countered.

The group murmured in agreement. Small lights twinkled in the trees above, where they relaxed on multiple blankets. They could hear the commotion of a party happening near the field they currently laid in. Bright stars coated the dark blue sky, and every few minutes a shooting star would soar above them.

"I'm not sure why I was marked as a clown. It's cool that you figured yours out though," Laura told Stella.

"You will too. It just happened in the moment for me," Stella replied.

"I think I know why for us," Adam said and looked at Elijah. Elijah wore his question on his face. "We had to learn to work together and hear each other out and stuff," Adam mumbled the last part, feeling stupid for even saying it in the first place.

"That makes sense," Elijah assured him, "we had to see each other differently." They shared a small smile.

"Everyone has a story," said Laura quietly. She was thinking about what Etta had shared about her life.

"Will we all stay friends?" Elijah asked quietly. He instantly regretted speaking and had hoped no one even heard him, but of course, Laura asked him what he meant. He explained, "We're all from the same town. If we ever go home, will we be friends?" He kept his eyes on his hand as he picked grass out of the ground.

"I'm down," Laura said. Elijah looked at her, surprised, and she smiled.

"I mean," Jaiden added, "we're the only ones who know what happened here. No one would ever believe us."

"True," Adam nodded. "You guys are cool."

Elijah smiled. That was the closest they would get to Adam saying he wanted to stay friends.

Stella chuckled, "Yeah, I guess you're alright."

26. A GIFT

"**A** handstand on someone's head?" Laura gasped.

Adam nodded with a mouthful of pancakes.

"Yeah, we've been practicing. Hank wants us to perform it in the show tonight," explained Elijah.

"I'm kinda nervous about the whole thing," Stella admitted, shifting in her seat.

"About messing up?" Laura asked.

"Yeah, and getting hurt. I mean, Nova could decide to be all rebellious at the last minute, you know?" Stella rubbed the lingering soreness in her neck from training.

"You're all gonna do amazingly!" Logan insisted. He had joined them for breakfast. "Everyone's always nervous for their first show. I threw up right before the first time. It was gross." Logan laughed along with the group. "But, you go out there and put everything you learned on display. It's such a rush. And if you mess up, it's okay. You do better the next time around."

Stella clapped dramatically. "You deserve an award for that pep talk."

"You really do, Logan." The group turned to face R.L. as he smiled playfully. "As soon as you're finished eating I have something to show you."

"The Door of Need?" Jaiden observed the distressed wooden door they stood in front of.

"Yes, the only door none of you have gone through in the Hall of Choice," R.L. leaned on his cane as he spoke. "Inside is a gift for each of you. Something to have for the performance. Are you ready?" The ringleader smiled wide, showcasing his slightly crooked front teeth. He turned and opened the door, ushering everyone inside.

"Interesting," Laura whispered. Her eyes raked over the five silver rectangular cases that towered over her.

The dimly lit room was empty except for the cases. The only illumination came from the floor that glowed with a soft white light. Each case had a symbol etched onto it that matched the markings on the recruits' arms.

Jaiden walked towards the one with a cannon on it. The door opened for him when he was only a few inches from touching it. The other kids followed his lead.

Stella gawked at the outfit that hung inside the case. She ran her hands over the tall black boots and traced the stitching of the white stars on them. She looked up to see black pants and a white jacket with a black star on each elbow.

Adam and Elijah looked at each other and then back at the navy blue full bodysuits. *At least no one we know will ever see me in this thing,* Adam reasoned. Elijah chuckled and shook his head, *only for Cirque,* he said to himself.

"I'm assuming we wear this for our performance?" Jaiden

asked R.L. He held a red helmet in his hand. A white *C* was painted on each side of it. The rest of his outfit was red leather pants with a matching leather jacket.

"You would be correct," R.L. affirmed.

Laura couldn't help but smile as she ran the colorful material of her costume through her fingers.

STELLA PEEKED through the thick curtain, the circus ring coming into view. The crowd was starting to fill in the bleachers, all with huge grins on their faces. Children begged for light-up souvenirs. Couples held hands. Lively calliope music came from the band. It was almost showtime.

"Breathe, Jaiden, breathe," Logan coaxed and patted his friend on the back.

Jaiden put his head in his hands. Barnaby had announced with a megaphone that it was thirty minutes till showtime, launching Jaiden into a panic attack.

I can't do this. I can't do this, Jaiden repeated in his mind. He suddenly felt like he did when he first started training–terrified, unprepared, and nauseous.

Arlo came at Logan's call and knelt in front of his trainee. Jaiden looked up to him with doubt-filled eyes.

"I can't," whispered Jaiden. He wiped his sweaty palms on his pants.

"Why not?" Arlo whispered back.

"I just can't," Jaiden hung his head again.

"Jaiden" –Arlo gently lifted his head– "you've been shot out of the cannon a dozen times now. You're amazing at it. You know exactly what to do. You've come so far. Don't let fear win. You have to change your thinking. Please, don't let fear win."

Jaiden contemplated. *I'm a shadow chaser. I'm a risk-taker. I'm the human cannonball.* With each thought, his breathing slowed, his body straightened out, and a smile slowly formed. *Shadow chaser, risk-taker, human cannonball. I was born for this,* he decided. Jaiden nodded emphatically.

"Atta boy," Arlo chuckled as Jaiden embraced him tightly.

"I'm the human cannonball," Jaiden announced loudly.

"Woo!" Laura hollered. She gave him a thumbs up.

"You ready?" Etta asked as she approached her.

"Yeah," Laura nodded, "I'm actually excited." She couldn't believe it, but she was. She wanted to get out there and make a complete idiot out of herself alongside her clown family.

Etta smiled proudly straightened out the bowler hat that Laura was wearing, "Give 'em a show, kid."

"LADIES AND GENTLEMEN," R.L.'s voice filled the Big Top. The crowd eagerly looked around, trying to find where the voice was coming from. "Boys and girls." Colorful lights darted across the people. "Children of all ages. Tonight we will steal you away from your world. We will invade your mind, your heart, and your dreams. Miracles will materialize right before your very eyes."

"He's so dramatic," Stella exclaimed over the noise of the audience cheering. Laura nodded and giggled.

"There's so many people," Adam gulped.

Jaiden and Elijah each surveyed the crowd and thought the same thing.

The kids continued to watch from the side of the circus ring, peeking through the curtains. Their nerves and excitement made it hard to stay still, but they couldn't take their eyes off of the production R.L. was putting on.

"It is my pleasure and my privilege." Adam took deep breaths. "To welcome you all." Laura squealed excitedly. "To Cirque." Jaiden bounced on the balls of his feet. "Des." Elijah said a silent prayer for everything to go well. "Élus," Stella laughed and clapped with the rest of Cirque backstage, performers and Side Show acts alike.

R.L. rode into the circus ring with a huge smile. He entertained the audience that cheered him on. He waved his top hat in the air as he circled the ring on his unicycle. He rode to the middle of the ring and introduced the trapeze artists as the first act.

Along with the recruits from backstage, the crowd watched in amazement as the trapeze artists performed their daring act. They flew and flipped and flung each other. Their performance had all the kids feeling very grateful they hadn't been marked with the trapeze.

"Stella, time to get in position," Julie told her.

Stella gulped and looked at her friends. Laura squeezed her hand reassuringly.

"You got this," Jaiden said matter of factly.

"Duh," Adam agreed. Elijah nodded.

"Thanks," Stella smiled and followed Julie to the horses.

Next up were the fire breathers. Annette marched out to the middle of the circus ring with them. They all wore black with their hair gelled back. Black painted swirls decorated their faces and arms. Powerful drumming was the soundtrack to their performance.

They threw and flipped torches of fire. The crowd gasped and dropped their jaws as they watched the fire breathers swallow fire and then open their mouths to release a huge flame that illuminated the darkened tent. The flames lit up the eyes of starstruck children and dumbfounded adults.

There was wild applause and cheers when the fire subsided, and the lights came back on. The group took their bows and left marching to the drums.

Laura and Adam laughed hysterically as the animal performers took the spotlight. The elephants, dogs, and orangutans doing tricks like riding bicycles, balancing on balls, and jumping through fiery hoops.

"Stella's up!" Elijah hollered as he saw the first horse come through the curtains.

Stella gripped Nova's reins as they galloped around the circus ring. The first time they went around, she stayed seated in the saddle like planned. She smiled and waved to the audience. Her insides were chaos; she was so nervous. There were two equestrians in front of her and Julie was standing in the middle of the ring as extra guidance for the horses.

The second time around the ring, all the riders jumped up to stand on their horses with their hands on their hips. The crowd's clapping sounded far away to Stella. All she could focus on was Nova and not falling off. Nova was doing amazingly. She was composed and exact in her movements.

The third time around, they all moved to stand on only one foot, alternating feet every several seconds. When they passed the curtains for their fourth time around, they were each tossed three silver hoops. Stella was anxious about this next part, but one look at Julie's confident expression calmed her nerves. *We've got this.*

All in sync, each rider slipped a hoop around their waist and started moving their hips to keep it in place. The other hoops were being spun one on each of the equestrian's arms.

Stella could've sworn she heard Laura squealing in joy and the boys hollering, but the crowd's noise would have definitely drowned their shouts out. But she smiled at the thought anyway.

When they passed the curtain again, each equestrian threw the hoops back and prepared for their finale. Standing once again with their hands on their hips, Julie nodded, signaling each rider to make their move.

Stella let out a deep breath. She grabbed onto the horn of the saddle and let her body fall but swinging both legs straight out to Nova's left side. Just as quick as the first time, she did it again, lifting herself to bring her legs to Nova's right side. Each performer did this in sync several times as Julie instructed the horses to move faster and faster.

And then, for the final maneuver, each rider held onto the horn of the saddle with one hand and brought their entire body hanging horizontally to the side of their horse that faced the audience. They smiled and waved to the audience as they galloped around the ring one last time and disappeared through the curtains.

27. A SHOW

"Alright, family." Etta gathered the clowns in a huddle. "Let's bring the laughter and keep an eye out for Laura. She's first of May. Let's help her out if needed." Everyone voiced their agreement.

Laura looked to Amos for an explanation.

"First of May means it's your first show. It's just circus lingo," he explained in a whisper.

All ears perked up when upbeat carnival music blasted through the tent. The clowns each let out a silly noise like a battle cry and headed for the curtains. Laura couldn't move until Etta pushed her forward. It took a minute for her eyes to adjust to the blinding lights. It was a good thing that the confusion she was sure was evident on her face, went well with her act.

The act they had planned was that Laura would be a sad clown and a skeptic to the silly antics of the other clowns. She wore a deep frown on her face, emphasized by the smudged red paint around her mouth. Painted on her forehead were two white triangles, one above each eyebrow. Gold glitter fell from her eyes like tears.

Every clown tried to make her laugh with their various acts, hitting each other with gigantic hammers, smashing whipped cream pies in each other's faces, 10 of them coming out of a very tiny car. The audience found it amusing how she kept the frown on her face and a disinterested look in her eyes.

The clowns acted more and more frustrated with Laura, making their efforts to make her laugh more ridiculous. It was getting hard for Laura to keep a frown on her face when the crowd was roaring with laughter.

Finally, the clowns decided to give up and leave their props on the ground and dramatically leave to the other side of the ring. The crowd laughed at the squeaky sounds of each stomp of an oversized brightly colored shoe. Like they practiced, Laura observed all they had left behind before picking up a red tube. She unscrewed the top of the tube and pulled out a bubble wand. Every move she made was slow and dramatic so the audience could keep up with her.

Laura furrowed her brows in confusion and attempted to blow a bubble. After two tries she finally blew a bubble that morphed into a giant lion that chased the clowns around the circus ring. The audience laughed hysterically at the clowns running and pushing each other out of the way. Laura continued blowing the bubbles, which shaped into elephants trying to stop on the clowns, birds flying over the audience, and even bubble clowns juggling.

By now, a small smile was on Laura's face. The final bubble was a bundle of balloons. She took a deep breath and thought back to their rehearsal before grabbing hold of the balloon strings. They start rising in the air, taking Laura with them. The audience's laughter got louder and louder as the clowns tried everything in their power to reach Laura and pull her back down to the ground, but soon she was almost to the top of the tent and laughing uncontrollably.

The lights went out at the top of the tent, and the music faded out as the clowns gathered their stuff and ran out of the circus ring as if to go and rescue Laura. R.L.'s voice spoke below, her introducing the next act. She floated to one of the trapeze platforms where Etta was waiting for her with tears in her eyes. Laura grunted as Etta pulled her into a bone-crushing hug.

"And now, my beloved audience, you will be flabbergasted at the physical feat of our next performers," R.L. waved his top hat in the air, "give a loud Cirque welcome to our astounding acrobats!"

Adam and Elijah came cartwheeling in with the other leaping and somersaulting acrobats. They smiled and waved to the bleachers and then performed their act perfectly. Even Elijah's handstand on Adam's head was done so well no one would've been able to tell it was their first show, except for Adam and Elijah, whose hearts were hammering in their chests.

They ended their act with a giant human pyramid. Elijah and Adam were on the middle tier, standing on the acrobats hands while holding up another person on their shoulders who held up the final acrobat. The lights went off, and they disassembled the pyramid.

As they ran back through the curtains, Adam and Elijah laughed and patted each other on the back, both thinking that the craziest thing wasn't the act they just performed but the fact that they were glad it was each other they were performing with.

R.L. stood on one of the trapeze platforms with the spotlight illuminating only him. "How are you enjoying Cirque des Èlus?" He asked the crowd with a booming voice.

Of course, he was met with wild applause and shouts.

"I am proud to present to you a daredevil act of a single performer!" A deep drumroll sounded. "Ladies and gentlemen, boys and girls—the human cannonball!"

The spotlight shut off of R.L., and another lit up the cannon in the middle of the circus ring. Jaiden stood in front of it, smiling and waving with one hand to the crowd while holding his helmet in the other.

I can do this. He hoped his smile was effectively hiding the mess of emotions he felt. He put on his helmet and began walking to the ladder of the cannon. After climbing up a few rungs, he turned and gave the audience a thumbs-up, causing them to clap and cheer.

Shadow Chaser.

Human Cannonball.

Risk-taker.

Jaiden repeated those things to himself as he continued to climb. He repeated them as he slipped into the barrel of the cannon. And he repeated them as he relaxed his body and heard the click of gears telling him it was time.

The sea of people smiling and applauding was a complete blur as Jaiden shot across the tent. The loudest sound in his ears was the rushing of air as he catapulted. The only thing that hurt was his cheeks from smiling so wide.

"It was insane, bro. You looked like a bird or something," Adam exclaimed. Jaiden laughed as he reclined on the couch.

All of Cirque was celebrating in the Commons. The Side

Show band was playing, and people were dancing and playing games. R.L. was currently beating everyone at darts.

"Were you scared you were gonna fall?" Elijah asked Stella as he stuffed a handful of popcorn in his mouth. They sat on the rug by the fireplace facing where their friends sat.

She shook her head, "Right before I was, but as soon as I did it, I was just so excited and lost in the moment. I was sad when it was over."

"I loved your thing, Laura. It was so funny and really clever," Jaiden said to her. She and Adam sat in matching armchairs facing each other. She was curled up with a quilt and he had his feet propped on the coffee table between them.

"And those bubbles were crazy!" Stella chimed in before taking a sip of hot chocolate.

Laura laughed and nodded. "Thanks, it was all Etta and Amos."

"Lies!" Amos appeared behind her. She jumped in surprise and then giggled. He leaned against the back of the chair. "You had everything to do with it! You were a natural. The crowd loved you!"

"I think I realized why I was marked as a clown," Laura said. She ran her thumb over her mark. "I don't need to be taking myself so seriously I need to slow down and be a kid a little bit more. I didn't realize how stressed out I was until I now. I feel relaxed at Cirque, like at peace or something."

"What were you stressed about?" Stella asked.

"My parents split up, and I'm just kinda caught in the middle," Laura explained with her eyes locked on her inner forearm.

The group nodded in understanding, all remembering their own stress at home. A wave of guilt came over everyone as they thought about their families, probably freaking out about them missing.

Amos leaned over on the back of the couch. "That makes sense. Be a kid, always. Even when you grow up."

"Very wise, Amos," R.L. spoke as he walked up to him. He patted him on the back. He surveyed the group. "Don't worry about what's going on at home. I can assure you that no one is worried."

They looked at him, alarmed.

"You can read our minds?" Adam gasped.

R.L. Snickered. "You're not my first recruits. It's natural to worry, but to your families, they don't even know you're gone."

"How?" Stella asked.

R.L. just smiled and changed the subject, "I know you've heard it a million times tonight, but you were all spectacular. I am so proud of you."

"It was crazy," Laura spoke.

"Crazy is our specialty." The ringleader winked.

"Hey, R.L.?" Jaiden sat up from the couch. "Have you always been the ringleader?"

"Yeah," Stella tilted her head. "How did Cirque start?"

"Did you grow up in the Circus?" Elijah added.

"It's quite a story," R.L. said as he sat on the couch.

"Can you tell us?" Laura begged.

"I suppose I can tell a little bit." R.L. smirked. He looked at Amos, who nodded excitedly.

Stella leaned forward on the coffee table in front of her, Elijah doing the same. Laura adjusted herself to be closer to the story. Adam took his feet off the table and rested his elbows on his knees. It was like the noise in the Commons became muffled as they waited for R.L. to begin.

"When I was a child, I was rather strange," the ringleader started.

"You? Strange?" Adam joked.

"Shh!" Stella demanded.

R.L. Chuckled. "I grew up in a place called Xul. It was a broken place, lots of hardship and cruelty and poverty," there was a softness in R.L.'s eyes as he remembered his childhood home. "I grew up in a kind family, but so many around me weren't as lucky. Ever since I can remember, I felt a pull to help. A fire shut up in my bones. A resolution in my soul to do whatever I could for those who needed it. Even if others felt like they didn't deserve it."

Barnaby approached the group and leaned over the back of the chair Adam was sitting in.

"Barnaby," the ringleader said with affection as he looked at his friend. "Barnaby is my oldest friend, practically brother. We both grew up in Xul, and we felt the call to make our world better. We left home and travelled to places worse off than our own. I was a builder back then, and Barnaby practiced medicine. So, I made repairs to buildings, houses, what have you, and Barnaby did what he could for those with sickness."

"What a time," Barnaby whispered.

R.L. nodded, "We met Clyde along the way, and he joined us. Clyde didn't have an easy life. A man of his stature with his gifts of storytelling and creating, he was rarely treated with kindness. The three of us traveled from city to city, having to leave due to being kicked out." The ringleader and Barnaby shared a chuckle.

"Why did they kick you out?" Elijah asked.

"People in power feared that what we were doing would cause the weak to rally against the strong. There were some dark and bad things taking place back then," R.L. explained.

"Still are," Amos interjected.

"That is unfortunately true," R.L. continued, "as we traveled, we met more and more of the people you see here today, Annette, Hank, Etta, Logan."

"Wow," Laura marveled.

"Did the Shadows exist back then?" Adam asked.

"They did. They were our biggest nuisance. We had many run-ins with them, lost some good people to them. To put many years of history into a short story, Cirque formed as we traveled together and did what we could to bring happiness, wonder, and peace to everyone we met. We eventually found the marvelous city of Ekklesia, and they helped us build a home here." He smiled at those around him. "And now we still help whoever and however we can."

"People like us," Jaiden marveled.

"Yes," R.L. affirmed. "People just like you."

28. A JOURNEY

The lights—red, blue, yellow—flashed as the carousel spun. The mechanical music played louder and louder with each turn. Red, blue, yellow. The horses, the tigers, and bears rose up and down.

Red, blue, yellow. Red, blue, yellow. The colors all smeared together.

Then, the colors started to slow down, and the music too. Slower, and slower and s l o w e r.

Until the carousel finally came to a stop.

"Jaiden? Hello? Jaiden!" Sophia waved her hand in front of Jaiden's face. He sat completely still, his eyes not fully registering where he was.

He took a sharp intake of breath and started moving his head around wildly. He was murmuring words under his breath that Sophia couldn't make out. He jumped up from his seat, not even looking at her, and stepped off the carousel as if he was searching for someone.

"Hey!" Laura yelled. Jaiden's head whipped towards her.

She held her phone and headphones in her hand and had the same worried, crazed look on her face.

"Why are we running so fast?" Stella's cousin whined as she pulled her and her brother over to Jaiden and Laura. None of them spoke. They just looked back and forth from each other.

Adam and Elijah jumped off of the carousel and ran to everyone. They all faced each other, Sophia and Stella's cousins watching from the outside, all baffled. The group took a moment to catch their breath and get their thoughts in order. Then, all at once, they frantically spoke over each other.

"What happened?"

"What did R.L. do?"

"How did we get here?"

"Is this for real?"

"What now?"

Another moment of silence engulfed them as they all remembered exactly what had happened.

"FIRE BREATHER, DEFINITELY," Adam answered.

"I think it'd be fun to be a Creator. Make the costumes and props and stuff," Laura chimed in.

"What are you guys talking about?" Logan asked as he joined them at the table. Lunch had just ended after a morning of sleeping in.

"What circus act we would want if we didn't get marked with what we did," Elijah explained.

"Side Show performer would be fun," Stella posed.

"Duh, we're the best," Logan bragged and howled, making the table laugh.

"What do you guys wanna do for the rest of the day?" Adam asked.

"We should go visit Ekklesia again!" Laura insisted.

"I'm down," Elijah agreed.

"We actually have other plans," R.L. announced as he approached the table.

"What are they?" asked Jaiden.

"Follow me," the ringleader instructed.

"Should've known that would be the answer," Adam said.

The kids kept up an excited conversation as they followed R.L. out of the dining hall. They walked through the halls of Cirque, through the Commons, and down a hallway they had come to know very well.

"Why are we going to the Side Show?" Stella asked as the ringleader opened the purple door.

He didn't answer but instead continued forward. The group shared a puzzled look. They followed him along the sparkling starry path towards the fire pit. The looks of confusion and worry grew as they saw their entire Cirque family standing together.

"Is this the part where they kill us?" Stella whispered to Laura, who just shushed her.

"What's going on?" Adam gulped.

R.L. Walked a couple more steps before turning and facing his recruits. He had sadness in his eyes but a smile on his face. A few performers behind him sniffled and wiped their eyes.

"It's time to say goodbye," was all he said.

The kids burst into questions and arguments.

"I wish I could have you here forever," R.L. silenced their outcry with his soft tone. "I am so proud of each of you. Someday you'll be back here to stay, but for now, home is where you are needed. For each other and for others who need to learn what you've learned here."

"But, we haven't even been here that long!" Stella fumed. She clenched her fists and ground her teeth together. She didn't mean to sound so angry but she couldn't help it. She wanted to scream and cry and throw a fit.

"We haven't learned that much," Adam added.

R.L. smiled at Adam's comment. "You are all so different from when you first arrived. You don't even realize the growth and change that has happened."

"But," Laura's tightening throat and bubbling tears wouldn't let her finish her sentence.

"Cirque has become your home and forever will be your home. Think of it as traveling somewhere to help people."

"Like you did," Elijah whispered.

"Yes, like we all did," he gestured to the crowd behind him. "We are family, and we've all gathered to say goodbye." R.L. stepped aside, allowing Cirque to gather around the kids.

"Come, child," Etta took Laura into her arms.

Laura couldn't hold back the tears now. She sobbed into Etta's shoulder. Amos hugged her next, and then all of the clowns. All giving her words of encouragement and trying to make her smile. Laura laughed through her tears.

"I'M NOT GOING," Jaiden informed Arlo. "I'm not. There's no way."

Arlo grabbed Jaiden by the shoulders. "You're gonna go home, and you're gonna be a human cannonball."

"What?"

"Figuratively," Arlo smirked. "You're gonna grow up and

find cannons. You're gonna find risks. And you're gonna take them. And when your family instructs otherwise, you're gonna remember Cirque. You're gonna remember our training, and you're gonna respectfully make your own decisions and pave your own way."

Jaiden's face scrunched up in emotion. Arlo pulled him into a hug.

"Now, LOOK." Hank looked between Adam and Elijah. "You boys better look out for each other when you get to where you're going. You understand?"

"Yes," Adam said.

Elijah nodded.

"I'm proud of you both," a few tears escaped Hank's eyes. "Elijah, your dad would be so proud of you." Elijah sniffled and wiped his tears away with the back of his hand. "And Adam, your dad doesn't know what he's missing." Adam looked at the ground, but Hank gently raised his chin, so they were eye to eye. "You're a good man. When things are rough at home, please remember that." Adam nodded.

"THANK YOU FOR EVERYTHING," Stella wrapped her trainer in a hug.

Julie squeezed her tightly. "I'll see you soon, Stella. Time goes by so fast. Before you know it you'll be here with Nova again."

Stella nodded and looked teary-eyed to her horse. She was beyond grateful Julie went through the trouble of bringing her here. She touched her forehead to Nova's. "Thank you," she whispered.

After a moment, Stella pulled back and looked at Julie. "Thanks for loving me."

She touched Stella's cheek lovingly. "You're worth loving, kid. It wasn't hard at all."

❖

The kids said goodbye to those they had come to call family. Logan howled in grief, causing the kids to laugh and cry harder. Barnaby gave them each a hug. Clyde hugged the group all at once with his giant arms. They turned to see their ringleader a few feet away, ready to lead them on.

R.L. walked the group past the train cars to the door in the tall hedge. Each kid gave one last look, remembering their first night here, feeling like it had been years ago and days ago all at the same time. They left through the door in the hedge and along the path they had walked when they first met the ringleader.

R.L. smiled as he remembered how they couldn't stop asking questions when they first arrived. But now, the moment felt too important, too heavy, to disrupt it with words.

The carousel came into view. The gold poles and fancy decorative trim on the top. The beautifully painted animals and murals that decorated the inside of it.

"It looks different," Jaiden mumbled.

"We're different," Elijah replied.

"In the best of ways," R.L. added. "Returning home will be difficult, but you're not alone." The kids looked at each other, knowing that no one would ever understand what they had experienced except for the people next to them. "When you return, you will see that time has not passed at all there.

You'll be right where you were. Nothing will have changed, except you, of course."

"How?" Stella asked. Her cousins would be on the carousel next to her?

R.L. just smiled, and they knew that would be the only response. He took a deep breath and hugged each kid, reminding them aloud of who they were.

"Equestrian."

"Clown."

"Human Cannonball."

"Acrobat."

Jaiden, Laura, Elijah, Adam, and Stella all stepped onto the carousel that would take them home, to that park, to their families, to the lives that they had wanted to escape not that long ago.

R.L. spoke his final words, and the ride began to move.

"Shadow Chasers," the ringleader declared.

AUTHOR'S NOTE:

I HOPE YOU ENJOYED THIS CIRQUE ADVENTURE. IF YOU TAKE ANYTHING FROM THIS STORY, LET IT BE THIS:

YOU ARE NOT ALONE.

SHARE THIS BOOK WITH SOMEONE WHO NEEDS IT.

AND REMEMBER, YOU HAVE A PURPOSE. YOU ARE STRONG AND SMART. YOU MATTER.

YOU, ARE A SHADOW CHASER.

National Suicide Prevention Hotline- TEXT 273Talk to 839863 suicidepreventionlifeline.org
1-800-273-8255

Youthline- TEXT teen2teen to 839863 - 877-968-8491

National Domestic Violence Hotline- 1-800-799-7233 - thehotline.org

Eating Disorder Awareness and Prevention - 1-800-931-2237 - national eating disorders.org

National Sexual Assault Hotline - 1-800-656-4637 - rainn.org

GriefShare - 1-800-395-5755 - griefshare.org

New Life Clinics - 1-800-639-5433 - newlife.com

United Way Crisis Helpline - 211 - unitedway.org

Focus on the Family - 1-855-771-4357 - focusonthefamily.com/get-help/

Alcohol & Drug Helpline- TEXT recoverynow to 839863 - 800-923-4357

Ourcirque.com - join our circus community through a free account.

CIRQUE AND THE SHADOW CHASERS
WOULDN'T HAVE HAPPENED WITHOUT

GOD.

MY FAMILY.

MY FRIENDS.

EVERYONE WHO READ CIRQUE.

THE AMAZING KIDS
WHO READ THE DRAFTS
AND HELPED MAKE IT
BETTER.

2020.

COFFEE.

ABOUT THE AUTHOR

Brooklynn Langston knew she wanted to be an author after reading *The Outsiders* for the first time in the sixth grade. The world of Cirque came to life in her mind during her junior year of high school. She published her first book, *Cirque*, in 2020. She currently lives in Jersey City, NJ and is working on bringing more stories to life! Follow her on Instagram @blangston27 and check out www.ourcirque.com

Made in the USA
Middletown, DE
21 April 2022